# BITTERSWEET SECLUSION

LAUREL JACKSON VANCE

WESTBOW
PRESS®
A DIVISION OF THOMAS NELSON
& ZONDERVAN

WestBow Press books may be ordered through booksellers or by contacting:

WestBow Press
A Division of Thomas Nelson & Zondervan
1663 Liberty Drive
Bloomington, IN 47403
www.westbowpress.com
844-714-3454

ISBN: 978-1-6642-9214-7 (sc)
ISBN: 978-1-6642-9216-1 (hc)
ISBN: 978-1-6642-9215-4 (e)

Library of Congress Control Number: 2023902409

Print information available on the last page.

WestBow Press rev. date: 04/20/2023

# ACKNOWLEDGEMENTS

I want to thank my family members for the encouragement they offered in helping me to finally complete this book.

A very special thank you to my son Tyler and my sister, Phyllis, for reading, editing, and offering suggestions for additions or changes to the story that might make it a more interesting read.

I'm ever grateful for the wonderful family God gave to me as they have edified my life in ways no words could ever sufficiently express.

I deeply love each and every one of you.

Laurel (Mom)

# CONTENTS

# PROLOGUE

Bittersweet Seclusion is the story of a young girl, Timarie Ellis, abducted by an unbalanced and dangerous individual, Marylynn Myers, and her two male "subjects" both of whom are mentally challenged. For reasons to be discovered, both are caught up in a web of illegal activities perpetrated by the abductor of whom they are forcibly indebted.

The young Timarie, experiences a variety of emotions throughout the story…everything from abject fear to light-hearted laughter. She plans an escape with hopes of finding her way home knowing that discovery by Marylynn will mean certain death.

Exciting and packed with mystery and wonder of what awaits around the corner. Will she find her way home?

The reader will undoubtedly find this story to be entertaining and unique from anything they've read previously.

## CHAPTER 1

# SUMMER PLANS

· · · · · · · · · ·

Ordinarily, at around 3:30 pm. each school day, the front door burst open and in would rush Tiffany Sanders. Today would be no exception. "Hi Mom, I'm home", she called out, as she marched into the kitchen, opened the fridge and peered in hoping to spot something appealing to snack on. The fact she was not really hungry at all wasn't the issue. Scrounging up a snack when she got home from school was just something she had to do. I suppose it was all about the comfort of just being home. After a brief over-view of her options, she decided nothing appealed, so she shut the 'fridge door and opened the freezer. Only one item was readily available, that being a box of assorted popsicles. She started to reach for one but then realized they didn't appeal, either. There was nothing else in sight except for several wrapped packages of meat and vegetables and other main meal items. Closing the freezer door, she sauntered over to the breakfast bar, perched herself atop the padded bar stool and decided to settle for a banana, peeling it back as she reached for the phone which hung on the wall next to the counter. She was just ready to dial her friend, Kara, when her mother called out from somewhere in the back of the house, "Tiffany, I'll be out in a few minutes. I'm scouring the tub." "Okay, Mom. No hurry." She was actually glad for the opportunity to speak with Kara privately while her mom was out of the room.

Kara answered after the first ring knowing it was Tiffany. "Hey Tiffany. Wow, haven't talked to you in a long time." "I know, huh? It's been at least an hour", said Tiffany, giggling. "Hey, we need to talk about our plans for after school tomorrow. I think it would be fun to walk to the mall. I happen to know that you-know-who plans to be there". "Oh my goodness, he is so cute." Kara replied, "I second the motion. But, is your mom going to allow you to walk that far?" "It's only a few blocks. I'll deal with my mom. It's high time she recognizes I'm not a baby anymore. After tomorrow, technically, I'm in 7$^{th}$ grade. And seventh graders require a bit more breathing room, you know? My mom needs to catch up to the real world."

By the corner of her eye, Tiffany noticed a shadow lurking near the doorway to the kitchen. Uh oh, that could mean only one thing. Mom had been standing there this whole time and heard everything.

"Oh. Hi Mom," Tiffany said with an extra bounce in her voice. I didn't see you standing there. "No, I guess you didn't." She stood there giving Tiffany one of those looks.

"Hey Kara, I gotta go. I'll call you later." "Okay, Good luck Tiffany. I have a feeling you're gonna need it."

Tiffany placed the phone receiver back up on the wall and then turned to face her mom. They made eye contact for one uncomfortable moment and then her mom said in a less than cordial tone, "You will not be walking to the mall, Tiffany. I will drive the two of you but you are not walking." "C'mon. What's the big deal? Walking with your friends is half the fun." "It takes only a moment for something to happen and you'd dearly wish you'd have listened to me." "But, there will be two of us. It's not like I'll be walking alone. Why are you so afraid?" Her voice was raised and tears welled up in her eyes. "Tiffany," her voice softened, "I cannot imagine life without you. If something were to happen...if someone were to come along and snatch you up, I could never live with myself for having allowed you to walk that far, even with a friend. Children disappear every single day and are never seen again or often times they are found...deceased. I could not bear it. It simply is not worth taking the chance." Now tears were welling up in her mother's eyes. She walked over to the window and stood quietly for a moment just gazing out at nothing. She was thinking...reminiscing.

Tiffany suspected something troubling had happened to her mother sometime in the past. Something she had not yet disclosed. She sat quietly on the stool waiting, hoping her mother might get around to sharing what was on her mind. What had happened in her own childhood that caused her to suffer such fear and trauma that she was reluctant to ever discuss it? After a few quiet moments, her mother turned and walked over to the dining room table, pulled out a chair, smoothed the back of her dress, and sat down. In a quiet voice she said, "Tiffany, I'm going to share something with you that happened way back when I was just the age you are right now. Maybe it'll help you understand why I'm so careful about allowing you to walk such distances." Now Tiffany knew for certain that something had happened when her mother was young but she'd never talked about it. Well, that was about to change. Her mother raised herself from the chair momentarily, walked over to Duchess, took hold of her collar and led the beautiful German shepherd dog out onto the back deck, shut the door and proceeded to re-situate herself at the table.

"Well, it all happened so long ago. But just like you are today, Tiff, I was at the end of my sixth grade school year. My best friend Trish, and I had been discussing our plans for the upcoming summer vacation. We were so excited.

Trish and I first met when we were about three years old. We immediately took to each other and became the best of friends. We were like little soul mates at a very tender age. Our mothers had signed us up for swimming lessons. Both our families had purchased new homes in the same neighborhood tract and nearly every home had a swimming pool. Both mothers had agreed they would never be able to sleep comfortably at night until their toddler was taught to swim. So, that's where we met. We lived about 4 blocks from each other and our mothers had also become very close friends, visiting and chatting, while Trish and I took our lessons.

Trish and I enjoyed each other's company so much so that our mothers looked for opportunities to allow us to play together. My mom would have Trish over while her mom went grocery shopping and vice versa. Or, one of us would stay at the other's house so our parents could enjoy an evening out on the town. Eventually, we started kindergarten together and remained just as close as if we were sisters.

Anyway, it was the evening before the last day of our sixth grade school year and we were so excited for summer vacation. Sixth grade was finally coming to an end. We were leaving elementary school and about to enter junior high. Back then, junior high included seventh, eighth, and ninth grades and we were definitely ready for the graduation to the upper grade level in a new school. It had become somewhat of an embarrassment telling people we were in the sixth grade and still going to elementary school. Both Trish and I were good students and were always at the top of our class. My favorite subject was language and hers, science. Our classmates often teased us, accusing us of being connected at the hip because they seldom saw one of us without the other.

Trish's dad was an attorney and mine, a building contractor. So, both families did well financially and as a result she and I wore the latest styles and had everything we needed and most everything we wanted, as well. And because of this, we were accused of being snobs. I don't really think we were. I think the reason they thought of us that way was in part because we preferred to keep one another's company exclusively. We had no desire to make close friends with anyone else though we were cordial with everyone.

I went to bed early that night eager to awaken to the last day of school. I had trouble getting to sleep because I couldn't relax and unwind. I must have gone to sleep at some point though because all

I remember is waking up to the annoying ringing of the alarm clock the next morning. To this day I hate alarm clocks.

Groggy and unwilling to open my eyes, it took only a moment to come to my senses and remember what day it was. I popped out of bed like a jumping bean and ran down the hall to the shower nearly knocking mother over as I passed her in the hallway. "Good grief Girl, what has gotten in to you?" she scolded. "Slow down!" I retorted, "Its the last day of school, Mom. I have to hurry so I can get there early for the yearbook signing. Oh, and Mom, would you mind dropping me and Trish off at school today? If we have to take the bus we'll have only five minutes to get in on the book signing before the final bell rings." A mild expression of irritation immediately crossed Mother's face so I quickly added, "Pleeease", and held my hands together as though praying. "Timmie, look at me. I look awful. I cannot go out in public looking like this and there is no time for me to get decent. Look at my hair," as she ran her fingers through her disheveled hair and then ruffled it. She let out a sigh, "Oh...never mind. I'll take you. I'll just cover my hair with a scarf. Go ahead, give Trish a call so she will be ready and waiting outside when we drive up." She walked away mumbling something. "Thanks Mom. You're the best!" I called out.

After calling Trish, I jumped into the shower and was finished in record time. I blew my hair dry with the hair blower then swept it up into a pony tail. I slipped into my faded blue jeans, pulled a baby-pink colored t-shirt over my head and put on my white sneakers. I was as ready as ever to meet the world. "Are you ready, Mom?" Mom shouted from the back room, "Peggy's gonna drive you girls to school instead. She said she's looking for a reason to take a drive in her new car. Saves me the trouble. She also said to have you ready and waiting for her out at the curb." "Okay, Mom...whatever. I'm headed out now." I quickly tied my shoe lace and headed to the front door kissing Mom's cheek as I hurried passed her. "Bye Mom".

As luck would have it, the sky was overcast. It was that time of year. Every June, California would be burdened with what they called "June gloom". It wasn't really cold out but it was cool...and no sun. I hated overcast days, most especially for today.

As I stood on the sidewalk watching for Trish and her mom to drive up, a beautiful car rounded the corner and slowly approached the curb in front of my house, parking right where I stood. Oh my goodness! There sat Trish in the front seat. The front passenger door opened and Trish jumped out and opened the back door for me as she gave a little bow and motioned with her hand for me to be seated. "Wow! Gorgeous car!" I exclaimed as I climbed in to the back seat. I remember it had that new car smell. The paint was a lovely red color. It was the prettiest car I had ever seen in my entire life, and I said that to Trish's mother. "Well thank you, Timmie. I kind'a like it, too. It's a 1970 Jaguar, first of its kind." "Wow, the last day of school and we get to arrive in style." Trish smiled proudly. "This is as good as taking a limousine, maybe better." I added with a grin.

In a few moments we arrived to the school and drove into the school parking lot. There were a few kids from our class already standing on the sidewalk handing yearbooks back and forth for autographing. Trish's new car caught the attention of several of the kids. They stood waiting to see who would exit the car and didn't look a bit surprised when it turned out to be me and Trish.

Trish and I had previously shared some silly ideas about what we might write in some of the year books. We knew we wouldn't have the guts to do it but it was fun to come up with silly, bright ideas. At the last moment I decided to go ahead and put some of those ideas to use. Jimmy Simmons handed me his book. I thought of how he always totally misbehaved every time we had a substitute teacher. So I wrote, "I'll remember you whenever I see a spit wad stuck to a ceiling. Have a great summer." I added a happy face. I told Trish, "His parents will probably read this and he'll finally be in trouble for it." We laughed. It was true, though. The ceiling above his head was plastered with them.

Then, there was Cindy Farnum. She was the only classmate Trish and I found to be unbearably annoying and couldn't bring ourselves to like. Still, we treated her cordially. My mother had taught me that if you can't say something nice then don't say anything at all. She also taught me that sometimes, the people that we find most unlikable are the ones who may need kindness the most. You never know what someone may be going through in their personal life. But Cindy was always coming to school with her double 'A' bra stuffed with toilet paper...or something. And then she would sit with her chest all puffed out trying to get attention from the boys. She didn't seem to realize that the boys in sixth grade were not likely to even notice or if they did, they weren't likely to care. We joked that we might write something like, "Hey Cindy, who knows...by the end of this summer you might just get lucky and fit into that double-'A' bra you've been stuffing all year." But, that wouldn't have been very nice so we didn't. Nonetheless, the thought brought some giggles from Tiffany, who was now listening intently to the story. They were interrupted by a scratch at the door. Duchess wanted to be let back inside. Tiffany hurried to the door just long enough to usher Duchess back in then re-positioned herself ready for the story to continue. Duchess ambled over to her water dish and noisily lapped up some water then retreated to her bed in the corner of the pantry.

Mother continued. "Soon the bell rang and everyone headed toward their own classroom. No complaints that day. Rather, everyone was ready for their class to begin. The sooner it began, the sooner the day would be over...for the whole summer. Each row passed their text books to the front of the class, as Miss Turner, our teacher, requested. Then, she told the class to take out our notebooks. "You will all need a pen. I would like for each of you to write a short essay about something your family plans to do over summer vacation. After that task is complete, I want you to jot down some thoughts on any topic having to do with something you may be interested in doing in the future. It may be career oriented, or just some goals you hope to achieve. Perhaps a travel destination. Believe it or not, you won't be children forever. There is no time like the present to consider the future. Do you plan on going to college? Do you hope to have a family someday? Maybe some of you hope to be a teacher...like me. This world could always use good teachers," she said with a smile. "You will be adults before you know it. Okay now, start writing. Take as long as you like. We have all day. Be creative and I want complete sentences. Correct spelling is a priority. Word usage and sentence structure is still an important objective. Just because you won't be graded on this paper doesn't mean you can forget all you've been taught. Show me how well you have learned. Make me proud." Miss Turner was a very positive thinker, an inspiring woman, perfect for the job of teaching children.

Miss Turner would be the only thing I'd miss about the 6th grade. She was a wonderful teacher...a wonderful person. So kind and patient. She was slightly built and thirty-ish. She had never married but seemed content as though she believed her only lot in life, her true passion, was to teach. She seemed genuinely concerned for each one of us and her methods of teaching made learning mostly fun. I loved her dearly...we all did.

As the class began one by one to complete their summaries, we were asked to stand next to our desks and read our essays aloud. As usual, as my turn approached, I could feel the blood rushing to my face from all the embarrassment. All eyes were suddenly on me and everything was quiet. I just wanted to crawl under my desk and hide.

I excelled in writing and was confident I had written a good essay but my shyness was getting the better of me. I did not know we were going to have to read aloud in front of everyone and I felt so unprepared. Timidly, I suffered through the reading and Miss Turner assured me it was very interesting and well written. Nevertheless, I was glad to be done.

The last hour of the day, we watched a movie about timber wolves. Their habits, how they hunt, raise their young, travel in packs and work together to subdue their prey. It was very interesting and informative. Last but not least, we had a class party complete with fruit punch, cupcakes, and cookies. It was fun. We laughed and made a lot of noise.

At last the final bell rang. It was time to leave. The school day was over. Our sixth grade year had come to an end. Then, it suddenly hit me. A chapter in our lives had come to an end. It was a bittersweet realization. This was it. We would not be returning next year as in previous years. No more Miss Turner. We would be moving on to an uncertain future and suddenly, it didn't seem so exciting. I felt sad and a bit scared. The reality of the moment overwhelmed me and tears welled up in my eyes. I looked at Trish and she too, was fighting back tears. In a moment, Miss Turner was at my side handing me a tissue as she placed one of her hands on my own shoulder and her other on Trish's. I grabbed the tissue, buried my face in my hands and tried desperately not to cry. Miss Turner offered some words of comfort, and that was all it took...the flood gates opened and tears rolled down my cheeks. Trish was crying too. I felt like such a sap.

In an effort to soothe our breaking hearts, Miss Turner said as gently as she could, "Aww, now girls. I cannot imagine the two of you wanting to stay here when you have your whole lives ahead of you. Life is just about to become a whole lot more exciting and interesting for you. I guess I could convince the Principle that you should both come back here next year. Would you like that?" The very idea brought me back to my senses and I couldn't help but smile as I looked up at Miss Turner. I said, "Not really, Miss Turner". We knew she was teasing.

"Well alright then. Let's dry those silly crocodile tears and get ready to go out and conquer the world. Never stop encouraging each other, keep those positive attitudes, and you'll do just fine. You know where you can find me if you ever need me for anything. And you'd better come back to visit now and then. Will you promise me you'll do that?" "Yes Miss Turner. I promise." Trish agreed with a sorrowful sounding, "Me too." We both gave Miss Turner a firm hug then turned to run for the bus. Her kind words and sweet sense of humor truly helped to sooth our sad hearts and I could almost swear that as she turned to leave, I saw her own eyes welling up with tears. She did not look back. I think I know why.

On the bus, things were back to normal...maybe even a bit louder than normal. The boys were loud and rude and as usual the bus driver was raising her voice to try and be heard as she demanded they sit down and be quiet. It didn't take long for me and Trish to get back to discussing our plans. It always took the bus a good hour to run the route, dropping almost everyone off before finally rolling to a halt at our bus stop. I was thankful that our journey was nearly over as our stop was coming up next. My stomach was growling from hunger and I knew what my first destination would be the moment I walked through the door...the fridge, as always.

Finally, stepping down off the bus, Trish asked, "are you going home or coming over?" "I'm going straight home. Mom just did some serious grocery shopping and there's some stuff in the fridge that's been calling my name for the last 2 hours. I must answer the call." I cupped my ear and pretended to be listening. "Can you hear it, Trish?" She giggled. "yeah, I'm kinda hungry too." "Well you know you can always come to my house and share in the bounty. We can raid the fridge together." "Naw, you know me, Timmie. I always go home and fall asleep first thing. Snacks are gonna have to wait. Mom says she thinks I'm going through a growth spurt with as much as I've been sleeping lately." "Wish I could say the same," I said. I'm beginning to think I'm never gonna grow. I've been a shrimp all my life and I'm probably always gonna be one. Daddy wouldn't know what to do if he couldn't call me "small fry" anymore."

Trish assured me she'd call just as soon as she woke up from her nap so we could continue our summer planning.

The bus stop was on the same corner that Trish had to turn on to get to her house. We gave each other a quick wave and started on our ways. I hated walking home alone. It wasn't really that far but I just didn't like it. Alone and hungry, I began to walk a little faster. I still had four blocks to go. Normally, it was a pleasant walk but when I was alone, it just felt creepy. The end of the street was a dead end. There was a six foot high block wall to my left which divided the back yards of the homes from the sidewalk rendering it virtually impossible to see into or out of the neighborhood back yards. Across the street to my right, there was a mostly dirt and weed field which spanned quite a ways back and a train track that was still in use daily. There were trees scattered throughout the field. Most were very large old pepper trees with huge, gnarled trunks. The branches were thick and bushy and hung very low to the ground providing a perfect hiding place for some hobo or a rabid animal or drug addicts. The thought made me cringe. Every day the train would come clapping through at about the same time. The whistle was almost unbearably loud and I'd cover my ears to block out some of the noise. I'd try to beat the train home but was seldom successful. Between the unpleasantness of the train whistle and the creepiness of the tree branches hanging to the ground, by the time I'd finally arrive at home, I had talked myself in to being so spooked that I would bust through the front door in hopes Mom would be there. Usually she was, but occasionally she'd still be out running errands and I'd beat her home. That was never good because when I was alone in the house, it would start making odd noises that I never heard when Mom was home. I could never go upstairs to change out of my school clothes because I was afraid someone would jump out of the shadows. It might be someone who lived out under those trees who was now hiding in my house. As soon as Mom would walk through the door all the scary thoughts and noises would disappear and I'd immediately run up to my room and change clothes.

Today, however, I noticed something unusual at the very end of the dead-end street.

Backed up to the field and facing my direction was a van, just sitting there with the engine running. It was difficult to see through the darkened windows but it appeared to be at least two people in the front seat. I had never seen any vehicle parked at the end of the street before. The occupants had been looking at me until they saw me notice them at which point they looked away and turned toward each other. My heart began beating faster as I noticed the vehicle begin to move, heading slowly in my direction. Now, they were looking at me. I tried reasoning with myself. Maybe they just pulled over to have a bite to eat. Maybe they're lost or just taking a rest. Then, as though on cue, the train whistle blew. At that moment the van began to move a bit faster and pulled up to the curb right next to me. I thought about running but my knees were weak and I thought I might hyperventilate. Why was I such a scaredy-cat, I asked myself.

The van stopped and the passenger window came down about half way. A woman sitting in the driver's seat said, "Can you tell us how to get to Magnolia Avenue?" I felt such a relief and I began to relax. Feeling a bit silly, I took a deep breath, and as I let it out slowly, said "Sure..."

Suddenly, the van's side door slid open and a man with very dark skin jumped out and grabbed me from behind. I forced out a weak, feeble squeal before his hand covered my mouth. The train whistle was still blaring loudly. No one could possibly have heard me. I fought as hard as I could, kicking and gouging his arm. Then, another man, a white man, emerged from the front passenger seat in order to assist the black man. He took a firm hold of my ankles and lifted me off the ground. My weak attempts to scream became nothing more than muffled sounds as my mouth was held tightly under the strength of his wiry fingers. They tossed me into the back of the van and then both jumped in after me, covering my mouth and nose with a cloth. I smelled a strange chemical odor and felt an odd sensation envelop my body, then everything went dark. I could no longer fight. All efforts to escape were futile. My body went numb. Just before I lost consciousness, I heard someone say, "C'mon lil lady. We don't wanna hurt'cha." I remember nothing after that.

# CHAPTER 2

# THE ABDUCTION

· · · · · · · · · ·

M arie Ellis busied herself in the kitchen. She heard the train whistle blowing in the distance and knew Timmie would be busting through the door at any moment. She continued chopping carrots and onions to add to the roast she was preparing for dinner. Tim Ellis would be coming home that evening from Sacramento and she planned to surprise him with his favorite meal...tender roast beef. He'd been out of town attending a convention over the course of the entire week. She missed him terribly whenever he was gone. She always made sure a surprise was waiting for him upon his return. Tonight would be no exception. After 15 years of marriage, Marie and Tim were still the light of each other's lives.

Marie had expected Timmie to burst through the door with a mouthful of stories to share about the last day of school. She was quite familiar with the routine. Timmie would invariably race to the fridge, pull open the freezer door and grab whatever was available that suited her mood at the moment. Marie looked forward to this time every day. She had always told Timmie that she reminded her of herself as a child and that watching her display such a zest for life was a special source of joy and entertainment for her.

She glanced at the clock. It was now 3:50. Timmie was about 20 minutes later than usual. She reasoned that since it was the last day of school, perhaps some of the kids lingered on at the bus stop to visit for a while and offer their farewells since they wouldn't likely be seeing much of each other until fall. She continued her dinner prep with little concern. A few more minutes passed and again, she glanced at the clock. *"Okay, this is getting ridiculous,"* she thought to herself. She was thinking that if Timmie wasn't planning on coming straight home after school she should have called by now...she knows the rules. Even when she goes over to Trish's house she knows she is supposed to call and check in. Marie expected the phone to ring any moment and to hear Timmie's voice on the other end of the line. She glanced over at the phone as though looking at it might cause it to ring. Then, another glance up at the clock. She wondered if Timmie missed the bus. But if that were the case Timmie surely would have gone to the school office and called by now. She reasoned that there must be an explanation for all of it and she would surely be finding out soon enough what it was. She pulled the cast iron Dutch oven out from under the cabinet and placed it on the stove. As always, she poured a small amount of vegetable oil into the bottom of the pan and ignited the heat beneath it. When the oil was sufficiently hot, she carefully placed the roast into the oil which produced a loud, angry sizzle and as always browned all sides of the meat, added a bit of water, some seasoning, turned the heat down very low and placed the lid on to the pot. In a few hours the roast would be juicy and tender and fit for a king...Tim.

She was just ready to pick up the phone and call over to Trish's house when the phone rang. 'Hello', she said in a less than friendly voice. But it was not Timmie as she had expected. It was Tim. "What's wrong, Sweetheart? I thought you'd be happy to hear from me", he said in a tone of disappointment. "Oh Tim, I'm sorry. I was expecting it to be Timmie. She still has not come home from school and I'm beginning to worry a little. I was just ready to call over to Trish's when you called. I'm not happy with her because she knows if she's going to be late she is supposed to call me." "Well, Honey," he said in a calming voice, "you know it's the last day of school. She probably just got caught up talking with classmates and forgot to call home. I'm sure you'll find her over at Trish's. Go easy on her. She's growing up and is bound to become a little more independent as days go by. She'll be okay." "Yeah, I guess", Marie sighed. "I'll tell ya what...I plan to be home by around 7:00. How about I take my favorite ladies out for a very special dinner. I would be honored if you would grace me with your presence, my queen." "Well, I would love nothing more than to accept your gracious offer but I already have dinner cooking on the stove. Maybe we can call a rain check for tomorrow night? I don't think you'll be too disappointed when I tell you what I'm cooking just for you." "Ahhh, don't tell me. Let me guess...pot roast?" "You guessed it." But Marie's thoughts immediately returned to Timmie. "I have half a notion to ground that girl when she gets home. I'll call over to Trish's as soon as we hang up. You have a safe trip, honey. I'll see you when you get here."

She abruptly ended the conversation as she was beginning to have serious concerns over Timmie. To put her mind at ease, she needed to get to the bottom of it and soon. She began wondering if her concerns were actually intuitions or could she just be over thinking the whole situation?

She depressed the receiver until she heard a dial tone, then lifting the receiver to her ear, dialed Trish's number. She began praying, "Lord, please let her be at Trisha's house and let everything be okay." Trish's phone began ringing, one, two, three times. Finally, Peggy answered..."Hello". "Hi Peg, it's Marie. Is Timmie over there? She forgot to call me." "I haven't seen Timmie, Marie. Trish came home and almost immediately went up to her room for a nap. I've been in the kitchen so I suppose it's possible she went up to Trish's room and I just didn't see her. Let me go check." Peggy laid the phone down and Marie could hear her scurrying up the stairs to Trish's room. She heard muffled voices and then footsteps coming back down the stairs. Out of breath and in a slightly frantic tone, Peggy retrieved the phone and said, "Marie, Timmie is not here. Trish said she left Timmie at the bus stop. She said Timmie was walking toward home last she saw her."

Fear gripped Marie's heart and chills enveloped her entire body. Her stomach became nauseous. She slammed the phone down without saying goodbye to Peggy and ran to the front door. She swung the door open, ran down the walk way to the sidewalk looking one way and then the other. She called, "TIMMIE!...TIMMIE!". When there was no answer, she ran back into the house and again grabbed the phone. She dialed 911. It rang on the other end a couple of times. "PICK UP...PICK UP" Marie repeated in a raised voice. Finally, a voice on the other end, "911...What is the address of your emergency?" Please...my daughter is missing and they want my address. "2402 Redwing". "Is that Avenue...street..." "Circle...please, Ma'am...my daughter is missing." By now tears were rolling down her face and she so wished that Tim was home. Everything would be so much better if he were here. He would know what to do. He always knew what to do. She needed his comfort and strength. He was always so stable.

"What is her first and last name, Ma'am?" "Timmie...Timarie Ellis." "Are you her mother?" "Yes." "Your name, Ma'am." "Marie, and my husband, her father, is Tim." Marie answered before she was asked. "She is not at her friend's house. I checked already." "Where was she last seen?" "Will you please just send some officers over to our house?" "They are on their way already, Ma'am. I just need to get some information from you for the record here. I'll be passing it on to the officers should it become necessary. May I have your phone number in case we become disconnected?" Marie obliged her with the phone number. The operator continued with a barrage of questions. Timmie's age, her height, approximate weight, description of her hair, what was she wearing?

Suddenly, the front door burst open and there stood Peggy and Trish. Peggy was crying and ran to give Marie a hug. "It's going to be okay, Honey. We'll find her," as she tried to comfort Marie. Trish's face was pale. She was crying and sobbing. She turned and ran up the stairs to Timmie's room calling out her name as she reached the top of the stairs and entered her bedroom. But there was no answer... no Timmie. Trish could not imagine her life without her best friend. Timmie had always been her rock, her very best friend in the whole world. She was stronger, more outgoing, more confident. Trish had always valued Timmie's strength at times when she needed some serious moral support. What would she ever do without her friend? She can't be missing, she just can't be.

There was a knock at the door. Marie glanced out the window. Finally, the police had arrived. A police unit had parked at the curb and there was a white unmarked vehicle pulling up and parking behind it. Marie was still on the phone with the dispatcher. She told the dispatcher that the officer had just arrived. She thanked her, hung up the phone, and hurried to the door. "Come in, Officer." She left the door open for the plain clothed officer who was on his way to the door. "Good afternoon, Ma'am. I'm Officer Davis. Detective Bill Shore will be with us in just a moment to ask some questions regarding your daughter. I will be in charge of dispatching officers to begin the search.

At that moment, Detective Shore appeared at the door. Marie ushered him inside then closed the door behind him. The detective offered his hand to Marie and introduced himself. Marie responded with her hand but was anxious to get on with the questions so the search for Timmie could begin.

He began, "Ma'am, I know that the dispatcher already asked you many of the questions I am also going to ask. I'm sorry to put you through it again. First of all, do you have a recent photo of her?" Yes. I'll go get it". Marie walked over to the fireplace and picked a framed photo from the group of family pictures displayed on the mantel. She opened the back and slid the picture out, handing it to the detective. There was Timmie, wearing a big smile. Her hair was draped to one side. Sandy blonde curls cascaded down one side of her face and onto her shoulder. Her soft brown eyes twinkled with a mischievous zest for life. The detective studied the photo for a moment and then commented, "... Pretty little girl." He then handed the photo to Officer Davis who took a look at it and then attached it to his clipboard. Officer Davis looked at Marie and said, "Ms. Ellis. An all-points bulletin has already been broadcast for your daughter. The Center for Missing Children has been notified. But for my own immediate record, I'll be asking a few questions that you have likely already given to the dispatcher. Timmie's full name and description, her age, friends, any boy friends, date of birth..."

"Timarie Justine Ellis. She's twelve, almost thirteen. Her birthday is September 2nd. Eyes, medium brown. Hair, light brown with blondish highlights. She's small for her age, about 4ft 9in. She comes up to about Trish's eyes. Trish is her best friend and the only friend she goes to visit. She has no boyfriend". Marie glanced over to Trish for confirmation. Trish nodded her head, no, and said, "she has no boyfriend." "How about birth marks...scars?" "Yes, she has a brown freckle on her right big toe. Also one on her inside palm, left hand and a strawberry birthmark at the nape of her neck," replied Marie. "What was she wearing?" "Faded blue jeans, pink t-shirt, white sneakers." All the recollections and discussion of Timmie had brought to the forefront of Trish's mind the reality that Timmie was truly missing and she began to sob. "Where and at what time was Timmie last seen and who was with her?" Officer Davis asked, as he fixed his eyes directly at Trish. He continued very gently, "Now Trish," he said, "I know this is all very hard on you but it is extremely important that you give me this information as accurately as you can." Peggy turned and put her hand on Trish's cheek. "Honey, you're going to have to pull yourself together...for Timmie's sake. This is very important." Trish wiped her eyes on her sleeve and cleared her throat in an attempt to gain composure. "Timmie and I got off the bus at the same location as usual. We waved goodbye to each other. I told her I'd call after I had a nap. I turned on to my street and she began walking toward home. That's the last I saw of her. Everything was just normal as it usually is."

At that moment, Officer Davis turned to leave, thanking Trish as he began to walk to the door. He motioned to Detective Shore that he was leaving. He needed to share the added information with everyone involved in the search for Timarie and get her picture out to the public. Detective Shore gave a nod and said, "I'll contact you as more information becomes available." Davis nodded and departed to his vehicle.

Only the detective remained. He hadn't said much until now. "Mrs. Ellis, I have been assigned this case. I want you to know that I have handled many, many, cases such as this. I have always been successful in locating the missing person. I will do everything within my power to locate your daughter. Here's my card. Don't hesitate to call if you think of anything that may be even remotely helpful. Sometimes it's the information that seems most non-essential that turns out to be just the information we need." He handed a business card to Peggy as well. "If you need to talk with anyone regarding the case, please call me directly."

Marie found herself studying Detective Shore. His looks did not impress her. However, his attire was neat and professional. He wore a tie and a sport coat. He was soft-spoken, older, slightly built with greying hair. She wished he had a larger build and a more intimidating countenance. His eyes were smallish, blue, and a bit close set. There was something about him that rang true, though.

His eyes had a look of intelligence and sincerity. His voice was the most intimidating thing about him. It was very low and he spoke slowly, with an air of confidence. She wondered if he shouldn't have been retired by now. Well, she was just going to have to trust him because for now, besides God Himself, he was her only hope.

"Is there a Mr. Ellis?" Detective Shore asked Marie. "Yes, there is." "Where is he? Does he live at this address?" "Yes, he does live here. He is out of town on business but is expected home tonight around 7:00." "What kind of relationship does he have with Timarie?" "They have a very good relationship. Timmie loves her father dearly and her father adores her." "Has Timmie been upset about anything lately?" "No, everything has been fine. She's been looking forward to summer vacation and going into 7th grade next fall. She would never run away, if that is what you are asking." The detective offered no comment in return.

The phone rang. Marie hurried to answer it. "Ellis residence. Yes, I'll get him for you." She motioned for Detective Shore to come to the phone. "Bill here. Okay...yes. I'm wrapping it up here now. I'll be right there." He hung up the phone, turned to Marie and said, "Mrs. Ellis, I want to assure you that everything that can be done is being done as I speak. We will keep you informed on any new information that comes in. We ask the same from you. Please stay home and near your phone. I'll be in touch with you momentarily."

The incoming call for the detective had been from Officer Davis. Davis had inspected the site where Timmie had gotten off the bus and followed the sidewalk for about four blocks, all the way up to where he found black scuff marks on the sidewalk. The dust that had previously collected on the sidewalk from the field across the street had obviously been disturbed by what appeared to be shoe scuffs. Thankfully, there were no obvious signs of blood anywhere around the crime scene. He strung yellow tape around the entire area and began taking pictures of items that were strewn about. There was a pink pencil with the picture of a white kitten on it, lying in the gutter. There also lay a shiny purple backpack on the curb. In the backpack was a small brush, a ponytail tie, more pencils, a lightweight sweater, a wallet that had two one dollar bills inside and a picture of Timmie and Trish, heads together, mouths wide open, laughing gleefully as though they hadn't a care in the world. A silver chain with a house key hanging from it lay in the gutter. He gathered the items, placing them in an evidence bag and presented them to Detective Shore as he rolled up to the curb and parked. Shore climbed out of his vehicle, examined the area and agreed that indeed, some type of scuffle had taken place here. He called Marie Ellis and told her he'd be returning momentarily so she could positively identify the items. Marie was waiting at the curb as he drove up. He presented the clear bag that held the items for Marie to examine. At first there was a moment of silence as Marie processed and confirmed in her mind the reality of the moment and then she began to sob. Her sobbing evolved into wails as she nodded her head, 'yes,' confirming each item found at the scene were indeed, her daughter's. She collapsed to her knees, hands covering her face. She cried out, "NOOOOO", as her most dreaded nightmare was being realized. She so needed Tim to be home.

Peggy threw her arms around Marie and cried with her, helpless to do anything else that might comfort her. Trish ran into the house and up to Timmie's room and lay on her bed, hugging her pillow, as she sobbed and prayed. "Please God, let Timmie be okay. Please bring her home to us."

Marie, suddenly struck with guilt, began blaming herself for the whole situation. Through her sobs she ranted, "I should have picked her up from the bus stop. Four blocks is too far for a girl her age to walk home alone. Why didn't I think about that? Why did I allow it? What is wrong with me? It's all my fault! My precious daughter is gone and it's all my fault," She began sobbing louder and uncontrollably. Her face saturated with tears as she continued crying loudly, blaming herself.

Detective Shore reached over and placed his hand gently upon her shoulder as he looked directly into her eyes and firmly stated, "Mrs. Ellis, look at me, LOOK AT ME! You cannot possibly blame yourself for this. Stop beating yourself up. No one could have foreseen anything like this happening, especially around here. There have been children taken right out of their own back yards before... even out of their own beds. Nothing like this has ever happened here before. If someone has determined to steal a child, they will find a way to do it no matter how careful you are." Then he softly added, "Now please...stop torturing yourself".

He waited for her to calm a bit then he asked, "Mrs. Ellis, when did you say your husband is due home?" "He is headed home by now," she sobbed. He'll be here in about an hour and he knows nothing about any of this. I have no way of contacting him while he is on the plane...and I need him here...I need him here with me now." She buried her face in a handkerchief and continued sobbing.

Officer Davis drove up to the curb near to where Mrs. Ellis was standing. He rolled the vehicle window down and as he leaned out slightly he said reassuringly, "Mrs. Ellis, I just want to let you know there is nothing to report as yet. But just so you know, the very best in the country has been assigned to your case. Detective Shore is the best there is. I want you to rest knowing that your daughter's case is in the most capable hands possible."

Detective Shore glanced over at Davis and nodded in appreciation then turned back to Mrs. Ellis. "Mrs. Ellis, I will return in an hour to meet your husband. Please stay near the phone". "I will," replied Marie.

## CHAPTER 3

# TRANSPORT

. . . . . . . . . .

had no idea how long I had been unconscious. I was beginning to awaken and tried to look around. I had no idea where I was. Everything looked so fuzzy. I couldn't focus on anything. I knew something bad had happened but could not recall the exact circumstances. I was incredibly tired but forced myself to stay awake. I squeezed my eyes shut and then opened them wide a few times trying to shake off the drowsiness. What had happened? My recall was slow in returning but a little here and a little there, and I began to regain some clarity. Oh yes...the van. Two men, a woman, asking for directions. I remember now...I have been kidnapped. I wonder what time it is? Does my mother know? Does anyone know where I am...who I'm with. Is someone coming to save me? A million questions raced through my mind and I began to cry at the mere thought of what my mother might be going through since I never arrived home after school. I whispered through my tears, "Mama".

My eyes were still blurry but I squinted trying to see my surroundings. I wondered where I was. The van was moving along the highway headed somewhere. Where were they taking me? There was a cloth covering my mouth that was tied at the back of my head. My feet were bound together at the ankles and my wrists were fastened tightly together with a plastic tie of some sort. I wanted to scream but didn't dare even attempt it. Even if I could have, no one would hear me aside from my abductors. I wondered what they would do if they discovered I was awake. They might kill me, I thought. I laid there silent as tears rolled out of my eyes and dripped onto the floor of the van. I tried hard not to make a sound as fear and sorrow welled up inside me and I felt compelled to cry aloud. Quite to my own surprise, a loud sob escaped my cloth-covered mouth and at once I began to cry full-on and could not stop myself.

No words of acknowledgment were uttered. It was as though no one had heard me. I finally gained control of my audible sobbing but continued weeping in silence. I concluded that if I was ever to be able to find a way out of this situation, I was going have to pull myself together and pay attention to detail and keep my head on straight. I had no idea what to expect. What were their plans for me? Maybe I'd never see my mom and dad again. Oh, the very thought sent chills over my whole body.

I felt the vibration of the road under the wheels of the van. I heard the sound of the engine and that swishing noise that happens when a vehicle passes nearby objects, like trees, large rocks, or vehicles headed the opposite direction. I felt as though we were on an incline and the road had become winding as I could feel my body rolling slightly to and fro as we negotiated tight turns in the road. I heard a window roll down just slightly and felt a sudden cool breeze. Then, I began to smell a familiar aroma. Oh, I know. It was the same smell as when Daddy took us on vacation up in the mountains. We had rented a cabin for the whole week. Trish came with us and we had such a wonderful time. We hiked, and fished, went horseback riding, roasted hotdogs and marshmallows. I was smelling the fragrance of pine trees. Yes, that's what I was smelling. It brought back such wonderful memories for just a moment. But this, this was an unwelcome reality.

I lay there on the floor of the van wondering what the future held in store for me. Then, a man's voice said, "Miss Marylynn, since the lil lady is awake now. What we s'posed to do?" A female voice, in a low, sarcastic snarl replied, "What...you think I don't know she's awake? DO NOT TALK!" "Yes, Marylynn."

I turned my eyes slightly upward trying to see who was hovering above me. I could feel the warmth of someone very near me and smell the stale breath. It was the black man who had jumped out of the van and grabbed me from behind. He had knelt to his knees and was closely scrutinizing me. His eyes met mine and I kept my gaze upon him, as well. His appearance was odd. One glance at him and it was obvious he was not altogether normal. A shiver went up my spine. He touched my shoulder with one hand and then with his other hand he touched his index finger to his own lips as if to say, "shhhh". He made no sound at all but remained completely silent while his eyes remained fixed upon me.

I could barely see the other man who was seated in the front passenger seat. He carefully glanced back a time or two but did not allow his eyes to linger on what was going on behind him. The woman, who was at the wheel in the driver's seat snarled, "Get up off the floor, Thaddeus. You are not to befriend anyone. You keep to yourself. Do you hear me?"

The black man began to raise himself up off the floor of the van but first he quickly pulled the corner of his shirt and gently wiped my tears. He smiled timidly and then set himself up on the seat behind me. "Yes, Miss Marylynn." "And you keep your hands to yourself too. Don't you be touching her." "Yes ma'am."

The woman's voice was cold and hateful. Who was she and what interest did she have in me? What were her plans? Her voice made me tremble and tears welled up in my eyes once again.

The other man, the white one, still had not spoken a word. I noticed him taking a quick glance back at Thaddeus, now and then, with a look of real concern. There was something different about these men. Both were odd looking and seemed a bit slow in their abilities. It also appeared they were under the woman's unyielding control as though fearful and beholden to her. They were afraid of her, understandably so. Everything about her seemed evil.

"Keep your eyes forward, Ernest." "Yes, Marylynn." She was watchful of every move they made and quick to bark out commands to which they immediately responded.

Meanwhile, the vehicle continued on a winding incline. Every so often we would pass another vehicle headed the opposite direction. I recognized the sound. The windows were too high up on the sides of the van for me to see anything. I wished that I could sit up in the seat so I could see where we were. From my vantage point I could see only sky. It was still light outside but was showing signs of evening approaching. Then, I noticed the rocky surface of a cliff and an occasional small pine growing out the side of it. There was other vegetation, as well. Small plants with little yellow flowers, weeds and brush of differing varieties. Yes, most definitely we were in the mountains.

I wondered how long I had been knocked out. It couldn't have been too long or it wouldn't still be light outside, unless...this was actually the next day. No...I think it's the same day.

My mind quickened back to my Mom, Dad, and Trish. My heart broke at the thought of what they must be going through. They had no way of knowing if I was alive or dead, where I was, who I was with, what was going on. Though I hated the situation I was in now, I was thankful just knowing I was still alive. I thought surely Mom and Dad must be looking for me by now. I missed Daddy so much. I hadn't seen him all week. I knew he would make everything okay. I began to pray silently. "Please God, help them to find me and please, please protect me." The very thought of Mom and Dad brought me to tears again. I began to sob. I tried hard to keep silent but the woman heard me. In a low growl she said, "Stop the crying." I fought hard to hold the sobs in. I tightened my lips together and turned my face to the carpeted floor of the van. The sobs continued but were less audible.

Suddenly, the brakes began to slow the van and I heard the

turn signal. The van came to a dead stop and I heard a car pass by going the opposite direction, we began to move forward again up a slight incline. This time, I heard gravel under the wheels and the van was moving much slower than before. Wherever we were now was heavily shaded by pine trees that occasionally brushed the side of the van as we passed near them. I guessed that we must be arriving at our destination. I heard the whine of the automatic window and felt a rush of cool, fragrant air as it blew through the opening and lifted the hair that had settled on my face. I heard what sounded like trickling water and smelled the dampness of wet sagebrush. Again, the van came to a stop. I heard the screech of rusty metal on metal. A gate rolling open, perhaps.

"Ernest, why haven't you oiled this gate? How long ago did I tell you to do that?" "Sorry, Marylynn. I did oil the gate but after it rains it seems to start all that screechin' agin." "Then oil it again this week." "Yes Marylynn."

We continued on and I heard the gate closing behind us. We traveled several more feet, and once again, came to a halt. This time I heard what sounded like my dad's automatic garage door. I supposed we were preparing to park the van in a garage. She proceeded and indeed, we entered a darkened garage. Once in, the door rolled shut behind us. The woman turned the engine off. A garage light had come on when the door opened.

We sat utterly quiet for a moment and then abruptly, she began to speak. "I'm going to say this one time so listen up. Don't anyone move until I have finished speaking and have given the order to begin. Thaddeus, you may remove the restraints from the ankles only, not the wrists until which time she is inside the house and you may remove the gag now. Ernest, unlock the kitchen door and accompany the girl to her room." The next comment was directed to me. "Young Lady, you may scream and cry all you wish now. There's no one around to hear you except us...and we don't care. However, if you wish to get along with me you'll conduct yourself in a lady-like manner and be ever so cooperative and that means...BE QUIET."

She raised her voice to add emphasis to her final wishes, then added, "I cannot stomach loud, annoying children. Now, get moving and do what I told you to do." Ernest proceeded to unlock the door and Marylynn disappeared inside the house.

Thaddeus took my arm and helped me to a sitting position. He gently removed the gag from my mouth and with a pair of scissors, cut the plastic restraints from my ankles. He didn't speak to me at all. I think he was afraid she might hear him. He had slid open the side door to the van, the same one he'd slid open when he first grabbed me earlier that day. I scooted to the edge of the open door and swung my legs over to allow them to dangle outside the van near the floor of the garage. He slipped out of the van and once standing, he took my elbow and helped me to a standing position. I felt light-headed and a bit dizzy. I began to lose my balance and he took hold of my arm to steady me. He whispered, "You okay lil lady?" I nodded, yes. I felt weak and unsteady but walked as he led the way.

The garage was separate from the house. As we exited the garage, we entered a covered patio area and then headed toward a door that was likely a side entrance to the house. Thaddeus continued guiding me toward the door. "Right dis way, lil lady." Ernest was waiting at the doorway and held the door open for us. We entered a well-organized pantry that led into a very large kitchen. Everything was clean and shiny. The appliances were all over-sized. Twice the size of regular appliances. We continued walking the expanse of the kitchen and were headed for some swinging doors. Ernest pushed through the doors, and again held them open as we entered a large dining room. There in the middle of the room was a formal dining table adorned with a beautiful, very large vase of silk flowers in reds, blues, and yellows. Other than the flowers there was very little in the way of decorations or frills. Similar to the kitchen, the dining room was immaculately maintained but void of any semblance of a welcoming atmosphere. There was no feeling or sign of anything that remotely resembled hospitality or warmth, at all. From the dining area we entered a living room. Like the areas of the house I had seen previously, it was large and beautiful. A lot of money had gone into the furnishings but again, no effort had been invested into adding a feeling of warmth or welcome. Mostly done in navy blues and silver, this room had a few pictures adorning the walls. On the far end of the room was a big fireplace made of white brick that spanned the entire length of one wall. A colorful vase and a few figurines adorned the mantle. Hanging above the mantle was a huge painting of Marylynn. There was a black, shiny, grand piano in one corner. Long, blue, velvet curtains were draped from the floor to the ceiling concealing the massive windows. The high camel-back sofa and love seat were a dark blue with a large, white, fuzzy rug laid at the foot of them. I wanted to stand there and study the room longer but we continued walking forward toward a spiral staircase. The staircase was wide at the base and grew narrow as it neared the top. Beautifully carved wooden banisters lined the stairs and continued on until they reached the top, then making a turn to the left became a balcony with the banister on one side only and doors on the other. Still no words had been spoken as we ascended the stairs. Finally reaching the top, there was a landing. There, hanging on the wall was a large painting of an elderly, distinguished-looking gentleman. We made the left turn to continue our walk toward the doors...three of them. We walked slowly passed the first door and then the second. I had to assume the third must be where they were leading me as there were no other options at that point. My heart began to race as I had no idea what was about to happen. My breathing became labored and I thought I might hyperventilate.

As we approached the third door we stopped. Ernest opened the door and motioned for me to enter. I hesitated but then slowly entered the room. Once inside, Ernest, having said nothing until now, spoke in barely more than a whisper, "Lil lady, please don't be afraid." His words were understandable but not very articulate. He spoke much in a manner that a five or six year old child whose abilities were limited might speak. He hesitated a bit between words and had a slight lisp. "Me and Thad will never hurt you. We will be caring for you while you are here. But you must not speak to us if Marylynn is around. She will be very angry if you do. We are not supposed to be friends with you...only care-givers. Okay?" "Okay," I agreed. "But why am I here?" "Shhh...Marylynn will talk to you about it tomorrow. For now, the bathroom is over there. This will be your room. You will sleep in this bed. There are pajamas for you in this drawer," he said as he pointed to the top drawer of a chest of drawers. "If you need anything, ring this bell," he said as he pointed to a bell with a string attached. I nodded. "Thad and I will be up in a little while with some water and dinner for you. But we have to keep your door locked at all times. Marylynn's orders." I just looked at him. At that, he and Thaddeus turned and left the room, locking the door behind them. Then, I heard the key reinserted into the door and the door opened. Thad, wearing a sheepish grin, reentered the room. He reached into his pocket and pulled out the scissors he had used to remove the plastic tie from my ankles and he reached for my hands. "Sorry lil lady, I almost forgot to take this off of you." He cut the tie and put it and the cutting tool into his pocket. My wrists were red and sore from the tie. I began to rub one wrist lightly. He picked up my hands and looked at my red, slightly swollen wrists then looked up at me. With a sad look on his face he said, "I'm awful sorry, lil lady. I dint know dey was so tight." I just looked at him and felt my eyes filling with tears. When he saw the tears stream down my cheek, his own eyes began to water. I didn't know who to feel sorrier for...me or them. So I looked at him and said, "It's okay, I know you didn't mean to do it."

It was a comfort to know that these two men had no intentions of harming me. Believing this did not soothe my fear of the woman they called Marylynn.

I began to peruse the room. It was not a huge room as what I'd seen from the rest of the house. It was about the same size as my bedroom at home though situated differently. The décor and mood of this room was entirely unlike the rest of the house. The atmosphere in this room felt quite warm and welcoming. There was a faint odor of moth balls. I wondered how long this room had been vacant. Though the room was clean and dusted, it didn't smell as though it had been recently lived in. It had a charm all of its own, however. The curtains which adorned the two gabled windows were ivory-colored crocheted lace. The quilt that lay across the bed was likely hand-made and was pleasantly colored in warm pastels. It bore a pattern of light green leaves with pink rosebuds perfectly positioned in the very center of the spread. This room was serene and feminine and sweetly decorated. In no way did it fit the character and coldness of my abductor. An oil painting of a shady courtyard, complete with a garden bridge stretched across a trickling brook, hung on the wall above the bed's headboard. A large floral arrangement of dried flowers set atop the antique dresser which was placed between the two windows. It made the room look delightfully Victorian. To the right of the dresser was a door which led into a simple but pleasantly decorated bathroom. Which reminded me...I was in dire need of the services of the bathroom. The bathroom was clean and smelled like a type of lemon scented cleanser had been used to disinfect it. I entered the bathroom and found relief at long last. As I sat there, I noticed white towels and wash cloths hung over the towel rack. A new bar of soap had been placed on the sink. A toothbrush, in an unopened package, lay on the sink alongside an unused tube of toothpaste. A medicine cabinet with a mirror hung above the sink, and there were drawers that I planned to inspect as soon as I could.

It was as though this room had been prepared for a special guest. I walked over to the drawers and slid the first one open. It contained a brush, a comb, a tube of lip balm, nail clippers, and a nail file. The next drawer had a hand-held mirror and a hair blower. In the cupboard under the sink there was a bottle of shampoo with matching hair conditioner, extra toilet paper, towels, wash cloths and soap bars. This bathroom was equipped and ready for a guest to stay for an extended period, as though they had been planning for me to come.

I was curious. Whose room had this once been? When would

I be seeing Marylynn again? What did she want with me? Oh, how I missed Mom and Dad. Would I ever see them again? And what about Trish? My eyes welled up with tears as the reality of my situation occurred to me all at once again.

Then I heard footsteps coming up the stairs. They were getting closer and closer to my room. Was this Marylynn? My heart began to pump wildly. I watched the door as though my life might hang in the balance. "Don't cry, don't cry", I whispered to myself. Marylynn had made clear how she felt about my crying. My breathing became labored and short as it had when we first arrived in the garage earlier. I heard the key in the door. It opened slightly and I could see the eye of someone peeking through the narrow slit. Then it opened slowly and wider until I could see it was Ernest and Thaddeus just standing there looking at me. It seemed a bit eerie at first but then I noticed they each held something in their hands. "Lil lady", said Ernest very quietly. "We've brought you a lil somethin to eat. It ain't much since we dint have time to plan much of a dinner. But it will keep you til tomorrow mornin and we'll bring you up a good breakfast. Okay?" "Thank you", I said quietly in return. They walked over to the dresser and placed the items down. There was a plate with a sandwich, a slice of pickle, and a bag of chips laid next to it. There was also a pitcher of water and a glass with ice in it and a single slice of pie on a separate saucer along with a fork. After placing the items atop the dresser they turned to leave the room. Thaddeus walked toward the door but Ernest hesitated. He stood in place and just looked at me. I wondered what was on his mind then noticed his chin began to quiver and his eyes filled with tears. He started toward the door then stopped to say, "We'll be back to see you in the mornin, lil lady. Marylynn wanted us to tell you that she will be up to chat with you tomorrow". They slowly closed the door and inserted the key into the lock. I could hear them quietly and slowly descending the stairs.

I didn't have a good appetite but I knew it would be best if I ate something. I hadn't eaten since lunch time at school earlier in the day so I proceeded to eat what the two men had left for me. I was thirsty and grateful for the water. The pie turned out to be apple, one of my favorites…and it was good. Once I finished eating, I laid down on the bed. The room was cool so I pulled back the covers and after removing my shoes, climbed between the sheets. I didn't bother to change into the pajamas that had been left for me. This wasn't home. I wanted to stay in my own clothes. It somehow made me feel closer to home. Daylight faded and had given in to night. The room was now dark. Exhausted, I quickly fell asleep.

## CHAPTER 4

# CONFINEMENT
# AND THE DIARY

· · · · · · · · · ·

Slowly, I began to awaken. The room was dim but I could see daylight coming through the window. I wondered what time it was. I had slept through the entire night in a state of unawareness of my predicament. I needed that rest. Perhaps I'd be better prepared to face whatever this day might bring and the impending visit from Marylynn. The birds chirped happily outside my window as though everything in the world was good and as it should be. If only they knew. Still, it somehow made me feel hopeful.

The room felt chilly and I pulled the covers up snugly under my chin. I needed to start thinking...thinking very hard about how I was going to free myself from my captors. Would I ever escape? I had no clue about what was going on. Why was I here? Where was I? What were Marylynn's plans for me? Everything was so unclear. I had nothing to go on. How does one make plans on a grand total of no information?

I prayed silently that God would help me.

Just then, I heard distant voices coming from downstairs. I listened carefully to see if I could identify whose voice I was hearing and what they were saying. Ah...it was Ernest and Thaddeus. They were quietly disagreeing as to which of them would carry what as they made their way up the staircase. Everything became quiet except for the sound of footsteps and then...a knock at the door and the key inserted. The door opened only slightly. The hallway behind them was dark and all I could see were two sets of eyes peering in at me. When they saw that I was not only awake but sitting upright on the bed, they continued on into the room. Both had wide grins on their faces and each carried in his hands covered plates with food items underneath. Whatever it was, it smelled heavenly. I had no idea how hungry I was until I smelled the food. This time they had a portable table with them, like a TV tray. They opened it, making sure that it was steady, then Ernest laid a white cloth over it before setting the food on top. Both were still smiling from ear to ear. "Are ya hungry lil lady?" asked Thad. "Yes, I am, very hungry," I said as a matter of fact. I figured that making friends with these two men might be the first step out of this situation, eventually. So, this was my only plan so far as I had nothing else to go on.

They always spoke very quietly when speaking to me. I knew why. Thaddeus seemed to be the most talkative of the two. "Did ya sleep okay, lil lady?", he whispered. "Yes sir, I did. Thank you." "We's brought ya somethin that we made jist for you. We hopes you like it." "I'm sure I will. It smells very good." Ernest removed the lid of the first covered plate. The aroma was amazing. My impulse was to reach for the fork, which I did. It was as appealing to look at as it was to smell. It looked like French toast with a strawberry and cream cheese topping. I didn't hold back. I dug right in and devoured the food. Honestly, I think it was the best French toast I had ever eaten. Maybe it was because I was so hungry. They watched as I ate, glancing back and forth at each other, smiling. "I think she likes it, Thad", Earnest stated as he stood gazing at my empty plate. Thaddeus nodded in agreement. "Yep, I think so too." They chuckled quietly. I decided that now would be as good a time as any to begin befriending them. "Did you guys make that yourselves"? They nodded, yes...big nods.

They over-nodded as they began to laugh and look back and forth at each other and then back at me. "Well, it was simply delicious. I never knew men could cook so well. That was the best French toast I have ever had." They were so flattered that they began giving each other high-fives and their laughing was getting a bit loud. They clapped and hopped up and down a bit. At that moment, a voice came from down the stairs. It was the voice of the wicked Marylynn.

"You two get those dishes gathered up, give her my message and get out of her room. What did I tell you was going happen if you start getting too friendly? GET OUT OF THERE RIGHT NOW!" she shrieked.

"Yes Ma'am. We's comin right now, Miss Marylynn," Thaddeus answered.

They quickly scurried as they gathered up all the dishes, wrapped them in the small table covering, then shot a quick look of fear my way before exiting the room. Before closing the door, Ernest poked his head back in and said, "Miss Marylynn wanted me to tell you that she will be up to speak to you before lunch time." I nodded in acknowledgment.

I heard the two men descend the stairs and as they reached the bottom I could hear Marylynn continuing her verbal attack on them. I listened intently hoping to pick up as much information as I could about her plans for me. But all she said was, "If I catch either one of you making friends with that girl, you're going to wish you'd never been born. Do you hear me loud and clear?" "Yes Miss Marylynn." they said in unison. "Now, get to the kitchen and clean up your mess." Without a word, the men quickly headed to the kitchen. I couldn't hear anything more after this. I wondered how these two men had come to be in this terrible predicament with this horrible woman. Eventually, I would find out.

I was alone now. I walked over to the window to get a view of the property that I hoped to eventually leave. It was a lovely day. The sun was shining. I opened the window just a crack. The window made a squeaking sound. I didn't want to make noise so

I stopped short of opening it more than just a couple inches. A rush of mountain air permeated the room with a most pleasant fragrance. The air was crisp...a bit too crisp but I left it opened a bit longer so I could listen for the surrounding sounds. I could hear the sound of cars in the distance. There were lots of pine trees on the property. The yard was large and had been landscaped to create a most interesting combination of forest and nature intertwined with a meticulously manicured courtyard, complete with colorful gardens and cobblestone pathways that led off into thick, tree-lined areas until I could no longer see their destinations. There, in the middle of a large circle of red bricks, surrounded by a lush rose garden, was a fountain with water spurting out an opening at the top. I then realized that the painting that hung over the bed was of this very scene. Someone had sat at this very window where I was now standing and painted the view. And there, off to the right, was the little garden bridge that lay across a babbling brook. The painted portrait was just as lovely as the actual scene. The likeness and beauty of both was uncanny. Somebody had some real talent. It made me wonder again, who had once stayed in this room?

I continued gazing out at the expanse of beautiful forested land. I was hoping to see the road that we had traveled in from. I could see the rolling gate that had screeched as we entered the property, but not the road itself. But, a little higher up through the trees as I looked out over the horizon, something sparkled like someone holding a mirror to the sun. I could only see an occasional sparkle. It was almost blinding at times. I wondered, is the sun reflecting off of a body of water...A lake, perhaps?

My quiet observations were brought to an abrupt halt as I heard the sound of footsteps coming up the stairs. This time, it sounded like only one set of feet and it was slower and more deliberate than the sound I had heard when the men were coming. My heart leaped and fear enveloped my whole body. I began to tremble and my breathing became rapid and shallow. What was she going to do? I had to get a hold of myself and calm down, fast. I mustn't allow my emotions to dim my ability to think. Daddy had always told me that "when things get tough in life, don't allow your emotions to run away with your common sense. You must always get ahold of yourself. Stop and think...THINK".

I must stay alert and take mental notes of everything she says to me. It may mean the difference between life or death...mine... literally. So, I took in a deep breath and slowly exhaled. I closed my eyes and tried to relax. To no avail.

I heard the key in the door and when the door swung open, there stood Marylynn. She stood straight and erect. Her face displayed no expression. Just cold, uncaring, like a shark. She stood silent for a moment looking at me as though sizing me up. Then she said in a quiet, slow, and almost monotone voice. "Young lady, we are going to have a talk, you and I. Not right this minute however, but later. I have things I must tend to for now. Upon our next meeting I will explain everything to you so you are clear on all rules and expectations where you are concerned. Once we have completed our conversation, you will understand what my plans are for you and I think you will like the situation once you have given it some thought. I will be out of town for a short period but will reconvene with you upon my return. Ernest and Thaddeus will deliver your meals and tend to any other needs you may have. One rule that must be adhered to. You are not to become familiar with Ernest or Thaddeus on a friendly basis. They are 'the help' around this place and that is all they are. You are not to mingle with or consort in any way with 'the help'...ever. You are to remain above all that. They know the rules, as well".

At that, she turned and left the room, locking the door behind her. I heard her footsteps fading off down the hallway and descending the stairs. I immediately began going over my mental notes. "Clear on rules and expectations that concern me? When I understand the plans, she thinks I'll like it?" Well, it doesn't sound like she intends on killing me...at least not right away. She would be "out of town for a short period"? I went to the window and peered out toward the driveway, which was to the far left of where my room was located. I saw a dark-colored sedan, perhaps a Cadillac, driving slowly toward the gate that we had entered through yesterday. I heard the screeching of the sliding gate and watched the car drive through it. It then slowly screeched shut. The sound reminded me of fingernails on a chalkboard. It was an awful sound and I could almost hear Marylynn cursing Ernest for not having oiled the gate.

I found a color book and a pack of crayons in the nightstand next to the bed. I hadn't colored in ages but what else was there to do? So, I opened the colorless pages and began to search for a picture that I could add some color to when I heard some noise from downstairs. Someone else must have been watching Marylynn leave as well because as soon as she was out of sight, Ernest and Thaddeus began a race that started at the bottom of the stairs and continued up to my bedroom door. Laughing and teasing, "I'm gonna beat you!" "Oh no you not!" till their bodies slammed against the door. "See...I beat you." "Oh no you din't", they laughed. I heard someone whisper, "Shhh!"

Then all became quiet for just a moment as one of them slipped the key into the lock. As usual, the door opened just slightly and two sets of eyes peeked in. I looked straight at them with a grin on my face. When they saw my amusement, they continued opening the door wide. With Earnest slightly ahead of Thaddeus, they both stepped in to the room. Since I was smiling, they both smiled as well and glanced at each other. One look at the other and they started laughing all over again. Their laughter was so light-hearted and genuine, that I couldn't help but chuckle. Every time they looked at each other the laughter would erupt all over again. Soon, we were all laughing...and we didn't even know why. It just felt good and I suppose it had something to do with Marylynn being gone. That would surely be a good reason for the men to be happy.

Eventually, the laughing faded and an awkward silence filled the room. They were trying to remember why they'd come to my door. It wasn't lunch time yet as it hadn't been that long since breakfast.

Apparently, they had just wanted to visit with the new guest in the house...just exactly what Marylynn had instructed them not to do. But who was going to tell? Certainly, neither of them...and certainly not me.

Ernest spoke first. "Lil lady, we just came up to visit with you 'cause we know yer all alone." Speaking to both of them, I said, "You know, you can call me by my first name if you like." Thaddeus asked, "Well, what is your name, Lil lady?" "Timarie. My name is Timarie." "I never heard that name before. But, I think we better keep callin' you "lil lady" because if Marylynn ever hears us callin' you by your real name, she gonna know we been getting' to know ya". Ernest was looking ahead. And he was right. It was plain to see he was definitely mentally challenged but mildly so. Thaddeus appeared to be a bit more challenged, I surmised after listening and watching the two of them. They were so friendly and cheerful and their presence did help pass the time. I decided it best not to ask questions about them and the situation yet. I didn't want to make them uncomfortable and have them stop coming to visit. It would be much wiser to become better friends first. It was plain to see that that was bound to happen. They treated me as though I were a very special addition to their lives and they were excited to have me around. Serving me and waiting on me was something they looked forward to doing. I supposed it was because I enjoyed and appreciated their efforts. What a strange situation this whole thing was. Through the course of our conversation, I discovered that Ernest was Marylynn's younger brother. But that was all I was able to learn this time around. Oh, how I wanted to launch into a question-and-answer session, but that would have to wait. I'd best be patient.

After a lengthy visit, Ernest spoke up. "Lil lady...we gotta go. It's getting' real close to lunch time and we got chores to do after we bring yer lunch to ya. Do ya want anything special?" he asked. "Oh, not really. I think I'll just trust your judgement." They both had big smiles on their faces and as they turned to leave, Thaddeus said, "I got a idea what we's gonna bring you. But it's a surprise. Can't tell or it won't be a surprise, right Ernest?"

Ernest smiled and nodded. The door closed, and then locked. I heard them challenge each other to another race as they headed for the stairs. The laughter began again as they rumbled down the stairs. It sounded like a small herd of buffalo. Once they reached the bottom, I heard them arguing over who won. If Marylynn only knew what was going on in her absence, she would surely be livid.

I commenced to picking up the crayons and thumbing through the color book. I found a picture that looked interesting that was begging for some color. As I colored, I began thinking about ways and means of getting out of this situation. I really couldn't devise a plan until I knew what Marylynn's purpose was for me. The only plan I could pursue for now is to make myself easy to get along with since I hadn't a clue about the actual situation I was in. It appeared as though accommodations had been made for me to be here for an extended period of time.

I was caught up in my thoughts as I sat coloring trying to recall anything my parents had taught me that might be helpful. But, I would have to think about all that later as I heard the two men approach the top of the stairs. This time they were not running. The key unlocked my door and then I heard a small knock. I said, "Come in". The door opened and they came in carrying a platter of food. It was a hoagie-type sandwich made with rolls, a plate of potato chips, something to drink, and a cookie. It looked appetizing enough and I hadn't noticed how hungry I'd become as I sat coloring and contemplating my situation. I set the book and crayons aside and stood up to get a closer view of the platter of food. I smiled as I looked up at the two. They stood in place waiting for a response from me...which I promptly supplied. "Wow, you guys. This looks so delicious. And I am really hungry." This time they had brought up a small chair for me to pull up to the vanity so I could use it as a table. Ernest pulled the chair back and motioned for me to sit. I dutifully sat, and he scooted the chair up for me. The plate had been placed on the vanity. They stood like perfect gentlemen waiting for me to take that first bite. Obviously, it meant a lot to them to see me pleased with their efforts.

So, I gently lifted the sandwich from the plate and took a bite. Thaddeus excitedly asked, "Well, lil lady, whad'aya think? I wanted to make you my very own favorite." I chewed for a moment until I was able to swallow enough to safely speak without spitting out particles of food. "I must say, this is the best tuna sandwich I have ever eaten in my life." It *was* a good sandwich though I used the opportunity to play it up a bit. It was heartwarming to see their reactions when I was pleased with them. They beamed with pride. Their mouths were open as though surprised and they looked at each other and did a high-five. "You really like it, lil lady?" "Yes, I really do. You guys are great cooks and you can make this sandwich for me any time you like. Thank you so much for your trouble." "Oh, you welcome, lil lady." replied Thaddeus. "I add just a little minced onion and chopped dill pickle to make it really good." "It surely does make it delicious. I'll have to remember your recipe." Thaddeus smiled from ear to ear, exposing his crooked teeth that included a large gap between the two top front teeth.

I wanted to get to know them better. The sooner we became closer friends, the sooner I could make plans. I was determined that I would, eventually, though I knew it would take time.

"You guys should sit down so we can visit for awhile," I said smiling. "It gets lonely being up here all alone." Ernest spoke up first. "Lil lady, we can visit with you for maybe a few minutes but we have work to do before Marylynn gits back. If our work isn't done, we git in big trouble. She whips us and screams at us, and plus, she never tells us when she will be back when she leaves. Sometimes she is gone for days but other times she comes back after just a few hours. So, we gotta get our work done soon." "Well, just so you know, she told me she'd be out of town for awhile." "Oh, so then we have a lil time to git our stuff done." They grinned at each other and high-fived. I went and sat on the bed so one of them could have my chair. Thaddeus quickly sat on the chair while Ernest walked over and took his seat on the other side of the bed. Ernest began the conversation with, "We really haven't been properly introduced to you, lil lady, so I will introduce us. My name is Ernest but Thad calls me Ernie". He then pointed to Thaddeus and continued, "His name is Thaddeus but I call him Thad." "So, do you want me to call you by your nick names?" "No, lil lady. Cuz if you do, then Marylynn gonna know that we been talkin'. She gonna think we bein' friends. So, you better just keep calling us Ernest and Thaddeus." "Yes, I see your point. Okay, I will call you by your real names. So, how did you two become friends?" "We been friends for a lot of years. Me and Thad knew each other when we were going to school. We went to a special school for kids that...well, that have learning problems. Thad's family used to make fun of him. He doesn't like livin' with his family because they're so mean to him. They always make fun of him jis cause he isn't smart...all except his Aunt Melba. She's real nice to him. He wanted to come stay with me since I'm the only friend he ever had. We're best friends and always gonna be. So, when Marylynn found out Thad wanted to live with me, she said, "Okay", But not because she was being nice or because she likes Thad, because she doesn't. She only said yes cause she can use him to get more work done around here. She is a very mean person and I wish I wasn't her brother. If I could go live somewhere else, I would. But I have nowhere to go. And, that's another reason that Thad wanted to live with us...so I won't be alone. When I told Marylynn that Thad wanted to live with us, she said, "That's fine. But if he's gonna park his black butt here, he's gonna be put to work right along with you." But Thad don't mind cause we're friends." "I see." It was all becoming clear to me now. Marylynn was the queen of this house and these two men were her slaves, her indentured servants..."the help." Since they had nowhere to go, no resources to leave, she could get away with using them to do anything she demanded...even help her kidnap someone. Sad situation for them. "I'm sorry that you are in this situation. I wish I could help you." "Thank you, lil lady.

You seem like a real nice girl" he said in a soft voice. His eyebrows furrowed as he was taking this conversation very seriously. In an effort to lighten the moment I said, "You guys can call me 'Timmie' if you like. That's what my parents and my best friend call me." "Oh no, remember lil lady, we better not do that. If Marylynn hears it, you know what will happen to us. You mustn't ever mention to her that you spend time with us...ever." "I won't. I promise." "And lil lady," he continued, "We're so sorry we helped Marylynn kidnap you. We din't want to, honest." "I know that now. I know it's not your fault. I totally forgive you. You are two of the nicest people I have ever met." They shifted their bodies a bit as they were pleased that I believed them and that I found value in them. They glanced at each other with a look of gratefulness and satisfaction that I still looked upon them with kindness after what they'd done. I admit, even though I meant what I had said to them, I felt a minor tinge of guilt as I knew I was schmoozing a bit in an effort to further ingratiate myself.

Finally, after about an hour of getting to know each other and having some very productive and revealing conversation, they decided it best to take the dishes to the kitchen and start on some of their chores. This was fine with me as I had run out of productive dialogue and was ready to rest up and digest some of the new information I had just learned.

After they left the room, I waited until I knew for sure they had vacated the general area, and I decided to do some snooping. After all, this was my room now so I figured I had the right to know what was here. I started with the closet. I opened the door to it and peered in. For being such a large closet, there was relatively little to be found inside. There were dowels for hanging clothes on either side of the closet. At the rear of the closet were shelves, probably for shoes and other accessories. There were also two larger shelves lining each wall above the clothes hangers to store larger items. I noticed there were a few assorted items resting upon those shelves. I grabbed the chair the guys had brought in for me and dragged it over to the closet.

I situated it so I could climb up and get a closer look at the items. There were some extra blankets folded neatly on top of each other. There was a pillow laid on top of the blankets. A kidney-shaped bowl and a bedpan set on the shelf near the blankets. But what I found most interesting was a pair of what looked like leg braces. They appeared to be made for someone fairly small...about my size. Again, I wondered who had been staying in this room. It must have been someone who was ill...a child...a crippled child. I noticed a couple of old books. I looked at the titles. "Answers to Common Questions About Polio." The other title was, "Pharmaceutical Medications Dictionary." There was also a little box. I opened it. It turned out to be a music box with a ballerina dressed in a pink tutu that twirled as the music played, "The Blue Waltz." The only items of clothing that were hanging in the closet were a light blue, flowered nightie and matching bathrobe. I left the closet and walked over to the chest of drawers. I had already seen what was in the top drawer...pajamas, underwear, socks, and the like. Nearly every item of clothing in this room was geared to accommodate a bedridden child. The chest of drawers contained three drawers in it. The second drawer did have a few shirts and a couple pairs of shorts. The bottom drawer had some pull-over sweaters and two pairs of pants. I wondered what had happened to this little girl. Where was she now?

I laid across the bed and my mind began to wander to home. Mom, Dad, Trish. I almost felt more sorry for Trish than I did myself or my parents. She relied on our friendship so completely. We were such close friends. I wish I could let everyone know I was alive and okay. I would contact them if I ever got the chance. I peeled myself off the bed. It couldn't hurt to check for a phone in this room. I'm sure, though, that a phone would be the first thing Marylynn would remove if there had ever been one here to begin with. I walked to the door and tried the knob. Of course, the door didn't budge. I knew it wouldn't but had to try anyway. I had heard them lock it as they left the room earlier. I searched the room for a phone outlet. There was none to be found. I thought about what Daddy might do in a situation like this. I knelt to one knee and prayed. "Please God, help me get home. Help Mom and Dad to be okay until they hear from me. Please help Trish and comfort her." I didn't know what else to say so that was it. That was my prayer. I only hoped God could hear me. If I ever needed Him to hear me, it was now.

I had no reason to believe, at this point, that Marylynn planned to kill me. I thought about how she had said she was going to inform me of what my "role" was going to be. Certainly, I could not fill a role if I were dead. As I knelt beside the bed, a thought occurred to me. I felt compelled to check for anything hidden between the mattresses. I lifted the quilt and slipped my hand between the mattress and box spring. I first slid my hand toward the head of the bed below where the pillow lay and felt around. I felt nothing, so I began to feel down toward the middle part. Still nothing. I forced my arm further in deeper toward the middle of the bed as far as I could. To my surprise, I felt something. I tried to grab it but had to reach a bit further to get a firm hold of it. It felt like a book. I carefully pulled it toward me until I nearly had it out. I listened for any movement or voices nearby before removing it completely. All was quiet so I continued. It seemed obvious someone had intentionally hidden it deep within the mattresses so it might never be discovered. I heard no voices so slowly retrieved it. It surely was a book. It had inscribed on it, "Diary." Oh, my goodness. I had hit the jackpot. I definitely did not want to get caught with this diary as I was sure Marylynn would confiscate it immediately. I would have to keep it carefully hidden as the person before had done. Perhaps now I could find out who was in this room and what had happened to her. I carefully opened it, feeling a bit guilty snooping into someone else's private thoughts and secrets. But I had to know what was in it and after all, this room was mine now, so, everything in it should certainly be subject to the new occupant.

The first date that had been submitted was roughly ten years from whatever today was. I had lost track of time and wasn't even sure what day it was. I began to read:

"Today is not a good day. I feel very ill but am trying not to worry Mommy too much. I told Mommy that I'm feeling better." I read a few subsequent entries, but then..."Mommy doesn't believe me when I tell her that Marylynn is evil. I told her that Marylynn hates me and that she said she wanted me to die. Mommy said I wasn't going to die because the doctor said I'm getting better. But my body hurts so bad. It is an awful thing to have polio."

New date entered: "Mommy says I need to stop talking sorely about Marylynn. She said that she's my sister and I should love her. I wish Mommy believed me. I do love Marylynn but she doesn't love me. And she doesn't love Mommy either. She even told me so."

New date: "The rain makes me feel so sad. Mommy is away today. She had errands to run and she left Marylynn to take care of me. My body hurts so badly and sometimes it makes me cry. Marylynn slapped me when I couldn't stop crying today."

I had only begun to read this doleful story of a terribly unfortunate girl who lay so ill in this very room, subject to the cruelty of Marylynn. My heart ached for her. I was anxious to know what happened to her. Where was she now?

My thoughts were rudely interrupted by the sound of Ernest and Thaddeus coming up the stairs. I had become so engrossed in the diary that I had lost all track of time. Hearing their approach, I jumped to attention slamming the diary shut and shoving it back between the mattresses as fast as I could and then quickly resumed my position on the bed, looking relaxed and bored. The sun had begun to go down and I hadn't even noticed. It must be dinner time, I guessed. I could hear them running and chasing up the stairs. This must be a ritual they planned to performed every time Marylynn was gone from the house. I had never heard them laugh and play like this when she was home.

But now, I could hear them hurrying up the hallway toward my room and finally they slammed against the bedroom door. "I won!"..."Nuh uh, I did." "Okay, it's a tie." They finally came to an agreement. I heard the key in the lock and as usual, before opening the door and entering, I saw two sets of eyes peeking through the cracked door. Once they saw I was awake, they entered, carrying a large plate of aromatic food with them. I hadn't thought about being hungry until I smelled the food. This time, they brought enough so that they could both sit down and eat with me. I was glad for the company. I could always resume reading at a later time. Heaven knows, it was looking like I would be here awhile. I would have to be careful not to mention anything I had read. I had questions to ask but in such a way they would never know I had read any diary at all.

They brought three plates and both began dishing out the food onto each plate. It looked like what Mom used to call roast beef with gravy. It was cut very thin, just the way I liked it. Also, green beans, biscuits, black olives, and something in a pitcher to drink. It tasted as good as it smelled. The meat was tender and tasty. I was glad they were good cooks. We sat and ate together without much conversation except for an occasional "Mmmm, this is good." They even included dessert...tapioca pudding, which so happened to be my favorite. Once we were finished eating and the dishes had been collected and ready to take to the kitchen, we began to have lighthearted conversation. We were actually feeling more comfortable with each other as though we were becoming closer friends. I never gave any indication that I hoped to ever leave the current situation. I didn't want them to think they needed to keep a closer eye on me than what they were already expected to do. I'm sure they were hoping I would be with them forever. Who knows? It may turn out that way but not if I had a say in it.

CHAPTER 5

# MARYLYNN'S INTENTIONS

· · · · · · · · · ·

S everal days had passed and many hours were spent hanging out with Ernest and Thaddeus. I had come to truly appreciate their company. They were always encouraging and cheerful. I don't know how they were able to maintain their good attitudes, given their circumstances, but they did. They were two of the most kindhearted people I had ever met. Maybe they just didn't know any better. It was obvious that as long as they had each other they would always be happy. God forbid anything should happen to either one of them.

Marylynn had been gone longer than expected...about 4 days. None of us minded in the slightest. In fact we all agreed it was wonderful to be at home without her. But as luck would have it, very late on the fourth night, I heard the gate at the end of the driveway slide open. That screech was unmistakable, and at night it sounded even louder than in the day time. She must have come in to the house and gone straight to bed because I never heard her moving around downstairs at all. Knowing she would likely be coming to see me in the morning made it hard to relax and go to sleep, but I finally did.

Following a restless night of tossing and turning, the dreaded morning finally arrived. I awoke at the first sign of daylight. The birds were loudly chirping, which didn't help because I feared they may awaken Marylynn. I looked out the bedroom window. I wasn't sure if it was mountain mist in the air or if it was the makings of an overcast day...which wouldn't be unusual for the month of June in California. It would become more apparent as the day wore on. I wanted to keep life in my new surroundings as normal as possible so I used the toilet, brushed my hair and my teeth and decided that today might be a good day to try on some of the clothes that were folded in the chest of drawers. I pulled open the second drawer where I had previously seen some folded shorts, pants and shirts. I lifted out a pair of pink pedal-pushers and shuffled through the shirts to try and find something that would match. I chose a comfortable looking t-shirt, white with black lettering that read HOLLYWOOD on it. It wasn't very pretty but I wouldn't be going anywhere anyway. I slipped the shirt on. It was a little loose but would do fine for just sitting around the room, which I assumed would be the highlight of my whole day. I pulled the pants on and they were too large. Luckily, they had a draw string around the waist that I could tighten so they wouldn't slip off. That worked out okay. I was as ready as I was going to be for a visit from Marylynn. Now, I just needed to convince myself there was nothing to be afraid of. I wanted to appear as confident as possible so as not to invite condemnation from her. Clearly, she was not the kind of person who took kindly to weakness. I wondered if I would have time to read the diary. My thoughts were dispelled by the sound of Thaddeus and Ernest heading downstairs. They were quiet, no words were exchanged between them. They weren't racing as they usually did, which told me they knew she was home. I guessed that they would soon be bringing breakfast and it would likely be shortly after that I would get a visit from Marylynn.

It wasn't but a few minutes that had passed when I heard the men coming up the stairs. They were quiet and much slower than usual. They arrived at my door and slipped the key into the lock.

As they entered, not a word was spoken. They wouldn't even look at me for fear I might speak to them and Marylynn would hear. They laid the food down on the table and scooted my chair over. As they were leaving, Ernest quietly said, "Miss Marylynn wanted me to tell you she will be up to talk to you when you're done eating breakfast. Please ring the bell when you're done." I nodded and thanked him but said no more. The breakfast was much less involved than usual. It was very basic. Scrambled eggs, bacon, sliced oranges, and a glass of milk. I gratefully ate the offering. My appetite was not what it had been yesterday morning. I rang the bell as soon as I finished so the guys would know they could come up and retrieve the dishes. They wasted no time in returning. I sat waiting, a bit anxiously. Marylynn didn't keep me waiting long. I soon heard one set of footsteps ascending the stairs. They were even and deliberate and I knew it was her. Once she reached my door, she stood quietly, as though thinking. It was creepy. She shifted her feet a bit and I heard the floor quietly creak.

Eventually, she slipped the key into the lock and the door opened. She stood gazing at me for a moment before entering, as though she was trying to intimidate me. Admittedly, I was intimidated but determined to returned the gaze and stubbornly kept my eyes squarely fixed on hers. Something told me this was what I needed to do to keep her from knowing I was afraid, though my heart was racing wildly. It was as though death was standing at my door. It felt indescribably eerie. I sat quietly waiting for her to break the silence. It seemed she wasn't sure how to begin. Finally, she said, "Good morning." "Good morning", I pleasantly returned. She looked me over from head to toe as she entered the room and set a bag on the bed. "These items are for you. I hope they fit. I assume the pants you are wearing you found in the chest. Obviously, they are too large. I am confident these items will be a better fit. What is your name?" "My name is Timmie." "Timmie?" as she raised an eyebrow. "Well, Timarie is my real name." "We'll have to do something about this. You will be "Loren" from here on...Loren Myers. Do you like the name, Loren"? "Yes Ma'am, I do. But I am perfectly fine with Timarie. It's what I'm used to." "It does not sound sophisticated. How did your parents arrive at such a ridiculous name?" "Well, my dad's name is Timothy and my mother's name is Marie." "I get it. But didn't they realize you'd have to answer to that name for rest of your natural life? Loren is much more suitable for a pretty girl like you. Naming you after themselves despite the repercussions was egotistical and selfish." She continued, "How old are you, Loren?" "I'm twelve, almost thirteen." "You're WHAT?" "Almost thirteen, Ma'am." "I heard you. You are entirely too small to be twelve. You are the size of an 8 or 9 year old. Are you telling me the truth?" "Yes Ma'am. In September I will be thirteen." "Well, had I known..." she said quietly as she looked down toward the floor, slightly shaking her head in disgust as she exhaled a deep breath. Clearly, she was disappointed. "And while we're at it" she continued, "DO NOT call me Ma'am again." She was annoyed. "You are to call me "Mother" from here on out, which leads me to inform you of why you are here. I am sure you are curious." "Yes Mm..." I caught myself just before letting it slip out. "Yes, Mother, I am." I noticed that she always spoke properly. Her speech fit her appearance. She seemed driven to display an air of absolute authority, intellect, and perfection.

"First of all, I want you to know that I have no intentions of hurting you. But, there will be rules you will need to follow." This resembled a threat to me, as though she had no intentions of hurting me UNLESS I stepped out of line. She continued, "You will not be allowed out of this room until which time I am confident you can be trusted not to try and run. I have no children. I always wanted to be a mother but my biological clock has run out, unfortunately. Even though, I really never had an interest in bearing children. The entire process is a rather nasty, demeaning, state of affairs for any woman to find herself in, not to mention the havoc it wreaks on a woman's body. My body is in excellent condition and I fully intend on keeping it this way. I always wished for a daughter, however. And now I have found one." Again, she fixed her eyes on me in what appeared to be an effort to catch some hint of a negative reaction from me. I offered no change in expression so she continued. "You're a bit older than I had hoped for but I feel as though you will do just fine. You're pretty. Any daughter of mine would have to be pretty. I carefully chose you. Yes. I had watched you for quite some time before choosing you. I observed you after school and how you related to your friends. I followed the bus and knew where you departed to go home. I knew when the last day of school was. Believe me, I observed several young girls and you were my special choice. You are special to me. Do you think we can be friends? Will you be my daughter?" Then, she held up her index finger, "Wait...Before you answer I need you to know these things I'm about to tell you. You will be living a very privileged existence. You stand to inherit much. This home, this property, everything I own. My ample bank account. You will be provided everything your heart desires and more. All I ask or expect in return is that you respect me. I need assurance of your undying loyalty, and confidence in the fact that you see yourself as no one's daughter but my own. To call me "Mother" is not too much to ask for what you will reap in return. It's a win-win situation for us both."

She became silent and was waiting for a response from me. At this point I realized that my very life, indeed, depended on my answer to her proposition. I hesitated and noticed she began to stiffen. I blurted, "It sounds like a wonderful idea. Yes, I will gladly call you "Mother" and I look forward to a wonderful future with you." I forced a smile. This woman was insane and I wasn't about to cross her or cause her to question my intentions. I realized, at this point, it would be imperative for me to hone in on any acting skills I might possess. My life truly did depend on it. I was deeply frightened by her but should never allow her to be aware of it. She slowly approached and bent over to embrace me. I reciprocated with a weak hug in return. It felt as though this embrace was the signing of a contract between us. It was a final agreement. From here on, I must do everything in my power to gain her trust. It was likely my only road to survival. As she stiffly wrapped her arms around me she said, "I think you will be happy here." "I'm sure I will be, Mother." At that, she smiled and turned to exit the room. "We will continue to keep the door locked until you become more accustomed to your new life...your new situation. It may take a while but we'll get there, eventually. I'm not a very trusting person so try to be patient with me. Agreed?" I nodded in agreement.

I had always heard that the eyes are the window to a person's soul. If there was ever any truth to that, I was seeing it now. There was no warmth in her eyes. Her eyes were expressionless...void of affection. Her attempts at feigning affection did not match her soulless eyes. She was cold as a glacier and it showed in her movements and her facial features. To her, people were nothing more than objects...possessions. They had worth only if she had need of them and they ceased to have worth once she was finished with them. Suddenly I realized that my thoughts and opinions of her were likely showing in my own expression. I smiled and gently replied, "I understand. It means a lot to me that you learn to trust me. I will try hard to be a good girl and be the daughter you have always hoped for." She seemed satisfied with my comment. I had no control over my continued evaluations of her. As I observed her movements and behavior it was fairly obvious she was in optimum condition physically. She was beautiful despite her icy demeanor. Her hair was dark auburn and was pulled back tightly into a French roll at the nape of her neck. No bangs, no hair on the face at all. She had beautiful dark brown eyes set perfectly below manicured eyebrows. Her makeup was meticulously applied but was minimal. She would have been beautiful even without it. She chose colors that complimented her hair and eyes. She stood about 5' 8"...tall, slender, and very toned. She had long, slender legs and a small waist. Her clothing was tailored and conservative but flattering. She wore a burgundy pencil skirt, knee length, and a white dressy blouse with black high heels that complimented her perfectly groomed appearance. She carried herself like a true professional; standing straight, shoulders never slouching, chin up, head held high, yet I had no idea what she did for a living or where she went when she left for days at a time.

Here I was, zoning out again as I focused on everything about her. I hoped she hadn't noticed nor taken offense at my gaze. So, I decided to lighten the moment with a comment. "I have just been noticing what a lovely lady you are and how beautifully you dress." She acknowledged by assuming a look of accomplishment and a mild air of conceit, slightly lifting her chin so as to put her nose in the air. She knew she was beautiful. She said, "Thank you, dear." She turned and left the room, but before closing and locking the door she glanced back and said, "I will return to visit soon."

My parents had often been amused at my uncanny ability to properly analyze people upon first meeting them. They were always amazed at how accurate my observations turned out to be. I think I had this woman figured out pretty well. Now, I would devise a plan to successfully tailor my relationship with her since I finally knew what this was all about.

I was just about to retrieve the diary from the mattress when I heard her turn back before heading downstairs. Again, she stood quietly before entering. I wondered if she was contemplating what she wanted to say and perhaps the best way to say it or was she just listening to see if I was moving about. I will never know. She opened the door and stood at the entrance. "...And yes, I do also wish for a son. I have never really been favorably inclined toward males but I suppose a family is never quite complete without one. How would you like having a brother?" I tried to hide the feeling of panic that swiftly overcame me as I knew full well what was meant by that comment. It meant most certainly, that she had the intentions of kidnapping another child in order to fulfill this wish. I thought quickly for the best answer I could come up with, hoping to diffuse her plans. "Well, Mother," relieved that I had remembered to call her "Mother", I continued, "With all due respect, I have always been an only child. I've never had a brother or a sister and I'm actually fine with that. I like boys okay but I enjoy being an only child, to be perfectly honest." I hoped I'd convinced her to drop the idea, and I dearly hoped that some family out there would not be missing a son before long. She stood in place with her eyes fixed on me for a moment. Then just before departing, she added, "Well... we'll see. I am proud to now have a daughter." I hoped that meant that she was willing to scrap the idea of finding a brother for me. She again entered the room and as before, she slowly approached me and reached out her hand to touch my hair, gently smoothing it and tucking it behind my ear. "You are such a pretty girl." And as she had already said before, "Any daughter of mine would have to be pretty" she said softly. "I think you'll be happy here. Don't you?" "Yes Mother, I do." She withdrew her hand and again, moved toward the door. Just before leaving, she glanced back and said to me, "You have a nice day, Loren. Oh, and just so you know, it is the responsibility of Ernest and Thaddeus to check on you every couple of hours to see to your needs. If they don't do as I have instructed, you are to report to me. I'll make sure it does not happen again. Agreed?" "Yes, Mother. Thank you."

She left the room, locking it behind her and finally descending the stairs. The house was quiet now. I stepped over to the window to see if she was leaving. I waited. In a few minutes, sure enough, there appeared a vehicle, backing out of the garage. This time, she was driving the van. My heart raced as I wondered if Ernest and Thaddeus were with her. The house had become so quiet I had to assume they were. This could only mean one thing. I knew that if they were home, they would be racing up to my door by now. I prayed, "Please God, don't allow Marylynn to steal another child. Please spare any more children this nightmare. Amen"

I heard the gate screech open and then close again. The house was now eerily quiet. I decided to take this opportunity to bury myself in the diary. I knew I was utterly alone so I reached between the mattresses and grabbed a firm hold on it. I found where I had left off and began reading.

"Today, Mommy is sick. She thinks she may have eaten something that did not agree with her. Maybe she did...with a little help from Marylynn. I think Marylynn wants Mommy to die just like she wants me to die. Mommy has been feeling worse and worse over the last few days. She never used to be sick. Now, she is sick every day. I worry about losing her. Who will I have to love and watch over me if Mommy goes away?"

"Mommy has not come to my room all day. That's not like her. She always comes to my room before she does anything. I asked Marylynn where Mommy was and she just smiled and didn't answer. I wish I could go to Mommy's room to see if she's okay. I saw Ernie and I asked him if Mommy was okay. He has quit speaking. I think he's terribly afraid of Marylynn."

"Today, Ernie's face is bruised and he has a swollen lip. I have not eaten all day and it is 9:00 pm. Ernie only brought me water but would not tell me why he didn't bring food. I think it's because of Marylynn. Maybe I will never eat again. How I wish Daddy was still alive. He would never allow Marylynn to do these terrible things."

"I can hear Ernie crying from his room. I have not eaten or been given any medicine for two days.

I heard Marylynn order Ernie to go with her someplace.

"I am very weak today. I have to stop writing. I hope someday someone finds this diary and reads it so Marylynn will be punished. I hope God punishes her. I think Mommy might be dead. I am so sad. I know I am dying, too. I want to go be with Mommy.

Bye, Ernie.

P.S. You have always been a good brother. I love you and we will see each other again someday."

# CHAPTER 6

# INVESTIGATION

· · · · · · · · · ·

etective Shore drove to the spot where the children normally got off the bus but that was not the actual crime scene. Yellow tape had been strung around the perimeter of the crime scene which was a few blocks up the street. The investigation was well under way. The crime had taken place approximately 10 yards or so from the corner of the street where Timmie would normally have made a left turn into her neighborhood. She had almost arrived at that point when she was abducted. The obvious struggle that had taken place on the sidewalk had, unfortunately, left few clues behind other than the items that had fallen to the ground that belonged to Timmie. About all there was left as evidence of a vehicle was a black rubber scuff mark on the side of the curb where a tire had rubbed the curb. There was also a skid mark where the vehicle had taken off in a hurry. Unfortunately, the tires had left no actual tread marks making it impossible to identify the make of tire on the vehicle. The shoe sole scuff marks made visible on the sidewalk offered no clue as to any approximate shoe sizes. The inspectors as well as Detective Shore had virtually no clues to go on. The television news had begun immediate broadcasts complete with pictures of Timmie and information on the abduction. The public was asked to keep their eyes open for Timarie Ellis. A phone number was furnished for anyone who had information to offer or should there be any possible sightings to report. Law enforcement had every reason to believe that Timarie was still alive but was being held by her captors. There was some speculation that this may be a ransom situation. All they could do was wait and see.

The evening was approaching as Det. Shore surveyed the area around the crime scene. As he was taking pictures of the surrounding area, a car drove up and parked across the street. Mr. and Mrs. Ellis exited the vehicle and headed in the direction of the detective. Det. Shore extended his hand and introduced himself.

"Mr. Ellis?" "Yes" replied Tim Ellis as he returned the gesture. I'm sorry we are meeting under such unfortunate circumstances." Tim Ellis nodded in agreement. He had just heard the news of Timmie's disappearance and the reality had not yet completely sunk in. "I'm Det. Shore, assigned to your case. I assure you everything possible is being done to track down whoever has taken your daughter. I need to ask you a few questions if you don't mind." "Not at all." "Do you know of anyone who might be responsible for this? Please give this question some serious thought. Do you have any enemies... anyone at all? At work, personal friends, acquaintances? Have you noticed anyone acting suspicious? Has anyone been watching your home? Have you turned anyone down lately who has asked to borrow money? Do you owe money to anyone?" Tim listened to each question, shaking his head, No, after each. He searched his memory for any information that may be helpful. The questions the detective was asking began to drive home the reality that his daughter was indeed, missing, and no one had a clue as to where to begin the search. All the obvious places had already been pursued.

Oh please...NO, Not Timmie! His pride and joy. The light of his life. Gone? Like a truck hitting a block wall head-on at a hundred miles per hour, he felt the sudden impact of reality. Tears welled up in his eyes. He looked over at Marie, grabbed her and pulled her to himself. Gazing into her eyes, and seeing the unbelievable grief looking back at him. That same grief that he, himself, was now experiencing, was too much to bear. This was real. He tried to hide his face from the crowd that had assembled at the corner of the street where his daughter had obviously fought with her abductors in a valiant but futile effort to remain free. He looked up into the heavens and cried out, "GOD...NOOO!" Tears ran down his face as he buried himself in Marie's neck and wept bitterly. This was a heart wrenching moment, not only for Tim and Marie, but also for their onlooking neighbors and others who had gathered, many of whom were also in tears as they witnessed the utter despair of the two loving parents whose child was now missing...maybe forever. Det. Shore was also deeply touched by this moment of sheer misery and despair he was witnessing. The thought of his own beloved granddaughter came to mind. He wiped tears from his own eyes as he removed a handkerchief from his pocket and then blew his nose. But then, a different reality hit him. He promptly set his own emotions aside realizing that he must focus on the investigation at hand. The more time that elapses without finding the girl, the less chance of finding her at all...ever. He set back to work.

"Mr. Ellis, If you think of anything at all that may be of help, please do not hesitate to call me. No matter how insignificant a thought it may be. There have been times when that one minor detail turned out to be the very piece of information we needed. I ask that you and Mrs. Ellis stay at home and as close to the phone as possible in case any information comes in regarding Timmie or if we have any questions for you. Here's my business card." He handed Tim two cards.

Tim Ellis wiped his wet cheeks, and with a look of pleading in his eyes glanced over at Det. Shore and asked, "Can I please be a part of the team and help find my daughter? I want to be there. I need to be there." Det. Shore replied, "I'm sorry, Mr. Ellis. I cannot allow you to do that. I wish I could. I truly understand how you feel, I'd feel the same. But the best help you can be is to stay at home with your wife. You will need the comfort and support of each other.

Please just stay near the phone. Tim nodded in reluctant agreement. "If we do call you with any updates, it will be very important to keep everything we tell you completely confidential. Repeating anything you learn to others could have a negative effect on the case." Again, Tim nodded in agreement.

Trish took notice of the evidence bag that was held securely in Tim Ellis' hand. She walked over to Tim and asked, "Can I see the bag"? Tim handed the bag to Trish. She studied the contents for a moment and suddenly, all color left her face. She turned pale and whispered, "Those are Timmies things. She really has been kidnapped, hasn't she? My best friend has been taken by someone. Timmie really is gone, isn't she?" Her legs began to buckle. Her eyes rolled back into her head and she fainted. Tim caught her before her body hit the ground and he gently laid her down on the sidewalk. Peggy rushed to her side, stroking her hair and gently coaxing her to wake up.

Tim squeezed his arms beneath her limp body and scooped her up off the sidewalk and began walking toward home, holding her as gently as he would a baby, or as if he were holding Timmie herself. As they approached the sidewalk to the front entrance of the home, she began to awaken. Tim laid her gently on the living room sofa, repeating to her over and over that everything was going to be okay. Trish just looked up at Tim as though she wasn't sure he believed it himself. "We're going to find Timmie, sweetheart. We're going to find her...I promise."

CHAPTER 7

# PUBLIC INVOLVEMENT

· · · · · · · · · ·

Without delay, reports of Timmie's disappearance had spread to every major television network, the local radio stations, and the newspapers. It was the news of the hour in all neighboring towns and counties. Soon, the news was spread to neighboring states in case the abductors had taken her across state lines. Timmie's parents had posters made up displaying her picture and these were attached to billboards, telephone poles, and fences all over the southland. Phone calls were beginning to flood the police department with people believing they may have spotted Timmie here or there. Each call was taken seriously and followed up on. Parents with children were more vigilant than ever, watching their own children more closely, worried that their child may be next. Neighbors were talking to each other and helping to keep a watch on any child that may be out playing. Churches were gathering for special prayer and candlelight vigils for Timmie and her parents. This unfortunate event was pulling people together in ways they had never known before. Everyone wanted to be a part of the effort to bring Timmie home safely.

Newspaper reporters had begun making a nuisance of themselves knocking at the Ellis' door and shoving cameras at their faces. Privacy at the Ellis home had become a thing of the past, and yet, the continual nuisance was a caring display of the public's concern that the Ellis' had to try and appreciate. Days had gone by and still no sign of Timmie, so the camera crews and phone calls were keeping the situation alive and in the forefront of the news broadcasts and public conversation. This was good as it would keep people watching for sightings and keep prayer chains going. New signs were showing up everywhere. "BRING TIMMIE HOME". "HELP FIND TIMMIE". The love and concern of the whole town was overwhelming. Cards and letters of love and support poured in to the Ellis' mailbox. It was wonderful...and exhausting.

Timmie's teacher, Miss Turner, paid a visit to the Ellis home in hopes of offering support to them in some small way. She offered words of comfort and shared the story of her interaction with Timmie and Trish on the last day of school just before they both boarded the bus for home. Her words to the Ellis' kept Timmie close, in a funny sort of way and kept their hopes alive. The media showed up at the house while Miss Turner was there. The moment they discovered who she was, they began pounding her with questions. Miss Turner was glad to answer questions and in so doing, take a little pressure off the Ellises.

"Excuse me, are you Timmie's teacher"? "That I am," she replied pleasantly. "What can you tell us about Timmie?"

"Well, I can tell you that Timmie is a very bright, delightful, and charming young lady. She comes from a wonderful home. She's friendly, outgoing, and warm-hearted. She is also a gifted student with a lot of good, common sense. I'm confident that her gift will be what helps bring her home. I pray her abductors treat her well and that she will be returned home soon...unharmed.

I wish to make an appeal to her abductor." She then turned her face to look directly into the television camera.

"On behalf of Timmie, her family, her friends...Please treat her kindly. We ask that you rethink what you have done and that you will not harm her in any way whatever. She is sorely missed by her family and friends and I would ask of whomever is holding her against her will, please, please, deliver her to a safe location so she can be returned home to her family where she belongs. She is their only child. Please show them some compassion by bringing her home. Thank you." She then turned her face away and dabbed her eyes with a tissue she had taken from her purse.

Again, the reporters began showering her with more questions but she was finished. She had nothing more to add so as she walked passed the Ellis', she told them she would stay in touch and for them to call if they needed anything at all. She proceeded to her vehicle, climbed in and slowly drove away, completely ignoring the camera crews as if they were invisible.

The investigation continued. All that could be done was being done. Shore had so little information to go on, but was doing everything he could to uncover any new clues or ideas on which to offer him a fresh direction to pursue. He drove over to the scene of the crime at the precise time Timmie would have been arriving there and he prepared to park at the very end of the street...the dead end, ironically, the exact spot the abductors had been parked. As he drove near the area, he noticed fresh tire marks. Someone else had recently parked there. He called the office to have an officer bring the kit that measures and takes molds of tire marks so they could get a measurement on the size and make of the tires. As he waited for the detective to show up, he heard a train whistle in the distance. He looked across the field past all the old, gnarled pepper trees and spotted the rail road track. The sound of the train was becoming louder and louder until the whistle, now blasting, had become so loud it could finally be seen heading this direction. He looked at his watch and wondered if this same train came through the area every day at this same time. Well, it certainly wouldn't hurt to contact the train company and schedule a meeting with the conductor.

## CHAPTER 8

# NEWS ANCHOR

· · · · · · · · · ·

Having read Carrie's diary in it's entirety left me with nothing to do in the hours I spent in seclusion, except to think and color. At least there would be an occasional break between the long, quiet, hours with the meals Thad and Ernie brought to me. And if Marylynn was not home, sometimes even a brief visit with them.

It was pretty safe to presume that Carrie was no longer alive. I wondered where she was and based on the information in the diary, she had not died of natural causes but at the hand of Marylynn. Where was the father...and, where was the mother? Carrie indicated that the mother may have been poisoned by Marylynn but she had not implied any foul play where the father was concerned. The diary had disclosed that Marylynn was actually younger than Ernie but because of his mental capacity, he posed no threat to her absolute dominance over him. From everything I had witnessed, she only kept him around because he was an asset to her. He was an employee that she did not have to pay. He was frightened of her so he never argued or offered up any defense on his own behalf. He just kept his mouth shut and did as he was told. As pay, he had a roof over his head and food in his mouth.

I was becoming closer friends with Ernie and Thad and was slowly gaining their trust. We had all become adept at pretending to be strangers whenever Marylynn was around. She was seldom home. I wondered where she spent most of her time and what she might be doing. I'd have to be patient. The truth would reveal itself eventually.

It was nearing lunch time and I could hear Ernie and Thad racing up the stairs as the usual. Their laughter was contagious and always made me smile. The key in the lock... and the door flung open. There they stood, plates and platters in hand. They always included lunch for themselves whenever Marylynn was gone. She must be gone because they had a big load of food on the tray. I enjoyed eating with them. It helped to break the monotony and invariably, I would learn a bit more potentially helpful information each time.

They opened the tv trays and laid out all the lunch options. They'd gotten pretty good at it as by now they'd had plenty of practice. We chuckled back and forth and offered each other all the usual accolades. Chatting was never difficult as there seemed to always be some news to share. But I was taken aback when Thad made an interesting statement. I thought I had heard him wrong so I said, "Wait a minute, what did you say?" He immediately repeated his comment. "I saw your mom and dad on TV last night. They was talkin' bout you bein' kidnapped and stuff. Your mom was cryin' tears and your dad was askin' for you to be brought home. "*WOW!* My heart dropped as I heard about my mom and dad being on the news. How I wished that I could have seen them. And how I wished I could call them. It had been at least a month since my disappearance and I was missing them so much. I had no calendar in my room so had lost track of time and days. There was no television in my room.

"You saw my family?" I asked as I tried desperately to hold back tears. Ernie answered this time, "Yes, Miss Loren. We saw your mom and dad." "Well, do you think they'll be on the TV again tonight?" "Maybe, Miss Loren." "I promise I will keep it a secret if the two of you will let me see them the next time they are on TV. I just miss them so much." Ernie and Thad looked at each other with hesitation. They knew that if they allowed me to come see my parents on TV, it would mean they would have to also allow me to leave my room and they had been given very specific instructions never to do that. So, I allowed my eyes to fill with tears hoping to appeal to their compassionate hearts. It worked. "Okay Miss Loren. If we see your parents on TV, and if Marylynn isn't home, we will come and let you see them, too." "Oh, thank you so much. You guys are the best." They loved feeling appreciated...thrived on it. "I promise you guys will never get caught. One of you can stand at the window and keep watch and I will only take a minute and then run back to my room. Pinkie promise!" I lifted my pinkie finger to intertwine with theirs. They quickly reciprocated and were happy and smiling again. Lunch was eaten and the dishes gathered and taken to the kitchen to wash.

Alone again and bored, I walked over to the window and looked down over the courtyard. There appeared Ernie and Thad each carrying yard tools. Clippers, pruners, rakes, and each began working at a designated area. Each concentrating on their own assigned tasks. The day was warm. Summer was in full swing. The house was quiet and I could hear the crackling sounds that an old house makes as it is warmed by the sun. I opened the window and felt the warmth of the outside air. The silence was soon broken by the sound of a lawn mower and then the scraping of an edger. The two workers continued for hours stopping only to gulp down water and wipe sweat from their brows. I observed as the courtyard took on a beautifully manicured appearance. Hedges so neatly trimmed. Finally, the task was complete. All trimmings were hauled off to a burn pile, the cobblestone driveway swept, and tools securely put away. This was a landscape job that should make Marylynn proud. The sprinkler system was set to go on and the lawn and shrubs were generously watered. The fragrance of the freshly mowed lawn mingled with the dampness and the smell of pines was delightful. I stood at the open window for some time enjoying the sight and breathing in deeply the fragrance of the completed work.

Suddenly, a dog appeared around the corner of the house. Ernie patted his thighs and called the dog over to him. The dog, tail wagging wildly, loped over to the men. Ernie and Thad petted his head and scratched his neck. The dog seemed to enjoy every moment of the attention he was getting. This was the first time I'd seen a dog on the property. There had been no barking or signs of any kind of a dog on the property before today. So his name was Princeton. He was a beautiful, very large, German Shepherd. Ernie glanced up at my window. I acknowledged by waving at him. He motioned for Thad to look up too. Ernie yelled, "His name is Princeton. He's Marylynn's dog, but we feed and take care of him." I smiled and nodded. They waved and the three of them disappeared around the corner of the lot. I thought of how fortunate I was to be in the care of these two disadvantaged but kind-hearted individuals. Things could be so much worse. I was convinced that because of these particular circumstances, I could actually work toward a plan of escape and find my way home...if I could just be patient, take it slow and use my head.

The days were longer now that it was summer time. It didn't get dark outside until close to 9:00 p.m. The house had been quiet since the men had finished the yard work. I had heard them come up the stairs but no laughing, talking, running. I assumed they had opted to take a nap before dinner after the hard day of work. Understandably so. But I was getting hungry. Finally, there was some stirring in the room next to mine. Someone opened a door and I heard some quiet discourse. Next thing, they were both at my door. "Miss Loren, are you awake?" "Yes, I am. Come on in." "Sorry dinner is so late, Miss Loren. We was so tired after working today we slept longer than planned. Are you hungry?" "I sure am." "Well, maybe tonight we can have something quick, like soup and sandwich, or somethin. Does that sound okay to you, Miss Loren?" "It sounds fine to me." In fact, it sounded really good. Most anything would have sounded good by now. It was a quick meal that I was grateful to receive. I had begun the practice of praying in thanks for my meals. The men seemed to like the idea. They always said, "Amen" at the end, right along with me.

After dinner, they retreated to their room again and I could hear the TV being turned on. It was 10:00 and I knew there was a news program that came on at that time. I could only hope that my parents would be on again. Especially since Marylynn was still gone from home. A few minutes later I heard them scrambling around and hurried footsteps coming toward my door. The door opened and both men trying to speak at once, excitedly. "Miss Loren...the news is coming on and they said that the Timarie Ellis case was next. Better hurry!" I had tucked myself in bed with a book I was not interested in. I threw the covers off and ran to the door. The bedroom right next to mine turned out to be Ernie's room. Both men watched TV there since there was no television in Thad's room. Thad stationed himself near the window to watch for any car lights that may come up the drive, and Ernie sat at the edge of his bed waiting for the commercial to end. I was anxious almost to the point of tears. This was the first time I'd been out of my room for...I'm not even sure anymore. Suddenly, there he was, a close-up of my dad, speaking to the cameras. "Our precious daughter has been missing now for almost 2 months. We have few leads and still no idea where she is. Please, don't stop looking for her. We have reason to believe she is out there somewhere. Please keep her in your prayers." Then the cameras focused on my mother who was standing beside to him. "Timmie, if you are somehow able to see us here tonight, just know that we love and miss you. We are praying for your safety and for your safe return home. We will never give up looking for you." Tears rolled down her pale cheeks and her voice began to waver as she spoke. She continued, "And to her captors, she's a beautiful, wonderful person. Please be kind to her." The mere sight of my parents compelled me to speak aloud to them. "Mom and Dad, I miss you so much. I love you. I wish you could hear me." Tears, streaming down my own cheeks. Mommy appeared to have lost weight. Her face was gaunt and her cheek bones were more evident than I had ever seen them.

A man in a suit stepped up next to my dad preparing to make his own statement. "I am Detective Bill Shore. Anyone who may know anything about this case, please call the number that shows up on the screen. If you see anything suspicious, or think you may have caught sight of Timmie, please call that number. I would like to talk to you. Also, there is a reward for anyone who shares information leading to Timmie's rescue and the apprehension of her captors." He then handed the microphone over to a reporter and the screen then focused on the television station anchor- person.

My jaw dropped when the anchor-woman turned out to be none other than Marylynn, herself. Ernie tried to usher me out of his room at this point but I insisted, "No Ernie. I need to see this." "But Miss Marylynn will kill me if she knows I let you see her on the news. I really mean it, Miss Loren." "She won't know, I promise." Marylynn began speaking to the public about the importance of keeping their eyes open for any clues as to the location and rescue of the missing Riverside County girl. So ironic that she would be the person reporting on the girl that she, herself, had stolen and had been keeping secluded in her own custody. Oh, what an evil woman. But through it all, I was learning more and more about Marylynn... just a little at a time. Now, as I observed her on the television screen, it suddenly hit me why she seemed to look a bit familiar to me each time I saw her. Though I was never one to watch the news, my parents did, so I HAD seen her before but just couldn't place where. This explained where she was spending a great deal of her time. She lived in the San Bernardino mountains but worked in L.A.. That's a long commute to make every day. So now, not only did I know what she did for a living, I also knew where she spent her time when away from the house. The pieces of the puzzle were coming together in a most interesting sort of way.

I had seen enough and Ernie was showing obvious signs of anxiety over my presence in his room. So I graciously thanked him for allowing me to see my parents and assured him that this event would never make its way back to Marylynn. I didn't want him losing sleep worrying about it. It was important that I not break his trust. I headed down the hall back toward my room. He looked relieved as he and Thad walked with me. Just before locking my door I turned to Ernie and said, "You can trust me, Ernie. I will never slip and say anything about this to Marylynn. Okay? Don't you worry about a thing." He smiled and nodded and seemed to relax a little. "Okay, Miss Loren'"

## CHAPTER 9

# DINNER WITH MARYLYNN

· · · · · · · · · ·

After about a week of absence, Marylynn came home. She seemed predisposed to spending her time alone. I wondered how she spent her time and where. I looked forward to the day I could tour the house and learn more about Marylynn.

Now, I heard footsteps coming up the stairs. I knew it was Marylynn because she barked orders over her shoulder at Ernie and Thad to bring dinner for two up to Loren's room. I was going to be eating with Marylynn tonight. I felt my shoulders and neck tighten and a feeling of fear came over me. My mind spoke to my heart to settle down and don't be afraid. I needed to look at these moments as opportunities to learn more about her. I knew that I was no match for her manipulative and clever ways to glean information. I would have to be on my toes and guard every word that left my lips.

I heard the key in the lock and the door opened. There she stood, without a word, just examining me, as was usual.

"I suppose I'm going to have to send word in advance when we will be eating together so you will know to clean up and have your hair combed neatly. How have you been, Loren? Is everything okay? Do you have need of anything, supplies, toiletries, shampoo... toothpaste?" "No, Mother. I have what I need, thank you."

She paused and then continued with more questions. "Let me ask you this. If you were to score Ernie and Thad on their attentiveness in tending to your needs, that is, the timeliness of the meals, the quality, etc. How would you rate them?" "Well, so far the meals have been timely and very good quality. They make sure I have enough water for in between meals and they leave snacks." "Do they come up often and bother you too much? Do they seem to want to linger and visit?" This was a loaded question. "No Mother. I only see them briefly when they bring meals up for me and then when they return to pick up the dishes. It would be fine with me if they would spend a little time visiting because it does get lonely up here sometimes." I was attempting to dispel any suspicions she may be harboring about the men and me becoming friends. She barked back, "Absolutely not! They are never to visit with you and you are never to suggest to them that they do. Is this understood?" "Yes Mother." "Have they allowed you out of your room yet?" "No, Mother. But it would be nice to be able to leave my room, sometime. I would like to see the house. I have been well-behaved and am settling into me new life quite nicely." "I will let you know when the time is right. But, perhaps I can figure out a way to provide some company for you." She gave me a look that told me she had something definite in mind. Immediately, I regretted saying anything about being lonely. It was too late to take it back so I tried to diffuse her plans by adding, "It's really okay, Mother. If I could just have some writing materials and maybe a few more books, I would have plenty to do and not be lonely at all. That would keep me occupied." Without looking at me, her only response was, "Hmmm."

There was a knock at the door. "Yes, what do you want?" She knew what they wanted but the power of forcing a response seemed to be an overwhelming need to her. "We brought dinner, Miss Marylynn". "Then, come in." The door opened and in walked Ernie and Thad. They spoke no words at all, just went straight to setting up TV tables, cloths, and removing lids off of serving dishes. When everything looked satisfactory, Ernie asked, "Anything else, Miss Marylynn?" "This will be fine, You may leave now." Without a reply, the two men turned and quietly exited the room.

I put on my very best display of manners that my mother had taught to me whenever we went out to dinner. I was wishing that I had listened and followed her instructions more carefully now. Marylynn did keep a curious eye on me. I saw through her subtleties. I supposed I did fairly well with regard to manners as she did not correct me on anything. We ate and chatted. I began to relax just a bit as she became more gentle in her subject matter and approach to me. She asked about my life, my friends, schoolmates, school in general. She was interested in my hopes and my personal interests. It became almost a pleasant experience.

We finally finished the meal and as she prepared to leave she said, "Loren, I thoroughly enjoyed our time together today. Let's do it again soon, okay?" I replied with a smile, "I would like that, Mother." She said she'd be sending the boys up to collect the dishes. She turned to leave closing the door behind her. I took a deep breath and let it out slowly. Just one more giant step to freedom. Getting to know Marylynn better and gaining her trust was my key. I felt good, like something was gained by our visit. I decided to shower, get into pajamas, and go to bed. I thought of taking the diary out and reading it again before going to sleep but decided it would be best to wait for a day when Marylynn would not be at home. No sense in taking unnecessary chances. Not to mention, it wasn't the type of reading material that helps one relax and go to sleep. So, once all was said and done, I just turned out the light, laid down, pulled the covers up under my chin and reminisced about Mom, Dad, and my dear best friend, Trish, until I became very tired. I said a quick prayer of thanksgiving and dropped off to sleep.

## CHAPTER 10

# ANTICIPATION

· · · · · · · · · ·

The sun shining through my window confirmed morning had once again arrived. It seemed as though I had just fallen to sleep. I heard the usual sounds of the local wildlife rummaging around for morsels of edible items for breakfast. Speaking of breakfast, my stomach was making its own noises. I hoped breakfast was being prepared. I rolled myself out of bed to take a look out the window. There was a squirrel running and leaping from limb to limb on the pine tree just outside my bedroom window. It was scolding and chirping as though annoyed about something. A bluejay screeched and flew off toward another nearby tree. The trees were full of activity and noisy as could be.

I heard voices from downstairs. Marylynn was already issuing orders to Ernie and Thad. Her voice, her very presence, was the only circumstance sure to ruin a potentially beautiful day. However, it also meant that breakfast was sure to be forthcoming, and soon. I heard no responses coming from them...Ernie and Thad. Surely, they were busy running to and fro in an effort to satisfy her unending list of tasks for them to complete.

Soon, breakfast was delivered to my room. There were no words spoken by either man as they entered and set up the usual table and placement of the food items. They were unusually quiet and serious. I knew better than to speak one word to them. Something was up...more than the usual stress from having Marylynn at home. For some unknown reason, Marylynn had succeeded in upsetting the usual routine. My curiosity was piqued and I could hardly eat for wondering what was causing the out-of-the-ordinary behavior. No sooner had I finished eating but they were at the door to collect the dishes. The only words spoken came from Ernie when he asked if there was anything I needed. I answered, "No", and without hesitation the door was closed and locked and the house was quiet once again. I sat in wonderment listening for anything I could pick up to try and put the pieces of this puzzle together.

About a half hour passed and I heard movement coming from outdoors. I peeked out the window and saw the white van backing out of the garage. My heart dropped. The sight of that van caused a flood of panic that grabbed my emotions. Tears filled my eyes when I saw Ernie and Thad disappear into the van. I was sure my suspicions were correct. The van descended down the long driveway and I heard the gate screech opened. A moment later I heard it close. A very dark feeling filled my heart as I knew that what I dreaded the most may be about to transpire. Was she on the hunt for a brother for me? Heaven forbid! I prayed she would be unsuccessful. I hoped I was wrong about all of it. Maybe it was just my suspicious mind working overtime. All I could do was wait...and pray.

I decided to shuffle through some of the books that Marylynn had given to the boys to deliver to me along with breakfast, hoping I may find one of them interesting enough to distract me from the current situation. I picked one and began reading. Then suddenly, it hit me. Among the stack of books were some that were obviously geared toward the interests of little children. I began to look through them again. These were not books chosen with me in mind at all. "Mother Goose Rhymes and Other Fairy Tales", "Assorted Children's Stories". She had something else in mind when she picked those books.

I decided to read the book I had picked for myself for lack of anything else to do. Since I couldn't concentrate on it, I ended up dropping off to sleep.

I awakened later in the afternoon. The house was still quiet. They had not returned home. I'd had no lunch and was hungry so I rifled through the snacks that had been left for me. Cheese and crackers, fruit, a slice of cherry pie. The house was too quiet and was making those crackling noises houses always make when you're home alone. When would they return? Even the animals and birds had become quiet. I rolled off the bed and walked over to the window. Still, no sign of anyone. I stretched, did a couple jumping jacks, did circles with my arms, walked around the room a bit lifting my knees high as I walked, in an effort to get a little exercise. This was the only exercise I'd had in what seemed like a lifetime. I lay back down on the bed hoping to fall back to sleep, but just then I heard the sound of tires on gravel. I leaped up and ran to the window and peered out. At first I saw no one but then I heard the gate opening and shortly thereafter, the van appeared, slowly rolling up the driveway. The garage door opened and then closed. All was quiet for a moment, then there were voices. I pressed my ear to the door but couldn't hear anything audible. I remembered a trick Trish had once shared with me about hearing better through walls if you place a glass to the wall and press your ear to the glass. I grabbed my drinking glass and pressed the open side to the door. I leaned in to see if I could hear anything. Sure enough, there was a faint sound of them entering the house through the kitchen door. I wondered if they had anyone else with them. A child, maybe? Now I heard voices but the words were not distinguishable.

## CHAPTER 11

# SUSPECT DESCRIPTION

· · · · · · · · · ·

D etective Shore was diligently seeking information but his efforts were met with one dead end after the other. He did, however, interview the train engineer who traveled through that area every day around the same time. It had been the same engineer working that route for many years. He said he'd recollected seeing a little girl walking, as he often did, while traveling through. Shore asked him if he had noticed anything out of the ordinary on that particular day. The engineer, seated on a stool, leaned forward slightly and began thinking back to that particular day. A moment passed, then he looked over at Shore and commented, "Oh hey, I do remember something. Probably not important but there was one day, around the time of the incident, a vehicle was parked at the end of that street." "Really? Can you describe the vehicle?" The engineer leaned his head back slightly and gazed up toward the ceiling. "If my memory serves me correctly, I believe it was a van. Light colored, maybe white." "Do you recall anything else?" "No. As you continue down that stretch of track, eventually a forest of trees blocks the view. I'm afraid this is all I can tell you. It's all I remember, anyway. Wish I could be of more help." "You've actually been a lot of help today. If you recall anything more, please don't hesitate to give me a call. No matter how small or unimportant it may seem, it could turn out to be the key information I'm looking for," he said as he handed him a business card.

This new information was immediately made public. The abductors may be driving a light-colored or white van. Each news station was anxious to be the first to share information that may aid in the rescue of Timarie and the arrest and apprehension of her abductors. Every station, that is, except Marylynn's. She found this new information to be distressing but was beholden to dutifully report it, anyway. She quietly reasoned with herself. After all, how many white vans are out there?...thousands. Her own van is rarely out of the garage. Nothing to fear. Just go on with life as usual. She couldn't afford to allow herself to be rattled. She remained zealous in her reporting, always remembering to encourage the public to remain alert for any information and new developments that may prove helpful in locating Timarie Ellis. She smiled to herself. *There is no more Timarie Ellis. There's only a Loren Myers, and no one is looking for her.*

Ernie and Thad had begun to make a habit of inviting me in to Ernie's room to watch the news whenever Marylynn was gone. They knew how much I missed my parents and they looked for any opportunity to make me happy. I had to remind myself often of how lucky I really was to have these two men as friends. But I must admit, watching Marylynn report on my abduction was infuriating. I hated her so so deeply and could hardly wait for the day I could expose her for who she really was. In the meantime, I needed to focus on being her daughter and winning her trust. Not an easy task under the circumstances. I felt like a liar...so dishonest. My life depended on my abilities to act convincingly. I had to view it as my form of self defense, an absolute necessity. I was determined to succeed, however long it took. Patience Timmie, patience.

News reports were beginning to slow down as no new information was surfacing. People were beginning to go on with their lives and think less about my absence. Everyone that is, except my parents and

Detective Shore. Shore was not accustomed to running up against such utterly impossible obstacles as he seemed to be experiencing on this particular case. He spent sleepless nights trying to figure out where to dig next. He'd sit at his desk during the day just thinking... forehead resting on his hand. He even took to praying over it. He was feeling like a failure. He believed he was letting my parents down but most of all, he was failing me. The weight of the world rested on his shoulders.

The less publicity on this subject, the more delighted was Marylynn. Her updates on it became nearly non-existent and whenever the rare occurrence presented itself, she kept it very short, simple, and toward the end of the broadcast. She was secure in the fact that eventually the whole situation would simply go away. "Unsolved, Cold files" was where this case was headed, hopefully, rendering her ever safe from discovery.

I so missed seeing my parents on the news broadcasts and oh, how I missed Trish. I knew that they would never give up hope on finding me. I had been gone now for 3 months. It was now September. My birthday, which was on September 2nd, had come and gone. A new school year would begin any day now...without me. Poor Trish. She would be alone now for the first time ever. The very thought brought tears of sadness to my eyes. I made a promise to myself to consult God for direction and protection every single day, and to remember my parents and Trish in my prayers as I knew they were praying for me. I just needed to be patient and trust that God would make things happen in His time. He had protected me up to this point. I was alive and well, plenty of food, protection, (so far) and had two friends that I knew would never hurt me. I would continue building a relationship with Ernie, Thad, and most especially, Marylynn.

CHAPTER 12

# SWEET BRADLEY

· · · · · · · · · ·

I t had become so quiet downstairs that I wondered if they had decided not to come in to the house after all. What was going on down there? Then, there came scuffling sounds and voices. As they neared the base of the stairway I thought I heard a muffled sobbing but I wasn't sure. I listened harder. When I heard Marylynn's sharp voice came through. "Stop your crying...right now!", I was sure.

My stomach dropped and I became nauseous...like I might vomit. They did it. They stole another child. I knew I'd better pull myself together, and fast. I'd best not allow any emotion to show that may trigger Marylynn to anger. There was no telling what she may do if she knew how angry and utterly disgusted I was over what she'd done. In her sick mind, she was bringing me a brother so I would have some company and not be lonely anymore. I didn't want to give her any reason to hurt this child. So, I took a deep breath and waited for them to come up to my room.

Just outside my door now, I heard Marylynn comment in as kind a voice as she could muster, "You're about to meet your new sister. You must be on your best behavior". Then, through gritted teeth she growled, "STOP THE CRYING." The key was inserted and the door opened but only Marylynn appeared at first. "Loren,

I'm not in the best mood. I'll make this short and sweet. You now have a younger brother. He is your responsibility. Of course, it will take some time for him to get used to his new surroundings. You will need to guide him in making this transition. Do NOT baby him. The sooner he gets used to his new home and family the better off we'll all be. Ernest, Thaddeus, carry on. Follow every direction as you've been given. I hope the presence of this child does not become one huge burden. Loren, you let me know if he becomes too much of a task." "Yes, Mother".

At that, Marylynn turned to leave. Ernie and Thad entered the room. Standing between the two of them was a very small child...a little boy. I would've guessed him to be around three years old. His eyes were red, swollen, and wet with tears. A strip of tape securely covered his mouth. He was sobbing uncontrollably and trembling. Knowing that Marylynn had left the area and was likely leaving the house, I told Ernie to remove the tape. "Slowly and carefully, Ernie. We may need to wet it if it is difficult to remove". Ernie responded immediately and the tape came off fairly easily though it left his cheeks red from the adhesive. Once the tape was off, the little boy opened his mouth and no longer held back his emotions. He began to wail from the depths of his soul. Oh, how he needed the comforting arms of his mother. I knew what he was feeling. I grabbed a blanket from off the bed, wrapped it around him and scooped him up into my arms. I sat on the edge of the bed, rocking him and crying with him. His wailing began to soften to an uncontrollable sob as his eyes were now shut and sleep was beginning to take over. He was exhausted. I laid his head on the bed pillow and covered him with another blanket, removed his little shoes, and swept back his brown curls from his forehead. I spoke softly to him. "Don't worry, Little One. I'll take good care of you. Don't be afraid. I will never hurt you. Shhhh, it'll be okay. He dropped off to sleep, but even in sleep, his sobbing continued. I went to the bathroom to get a rag wet with warm water to gently wipe his face and eyes. He remained asleep.

I glanced up at Ernie and Thad who had both been standing

there observing my every move. Both their faces, wet with tears. "We're so sorry, Timmie", Thad sobbed. I answered, "You must remember not to call me "Timmie", Thad. Always call me Loren. You know what will happen if Marylynn ever hears you." "Yes, Miss Loren". "Do either of you happen to know his name?" "No, Miss Loren", Ernie replied. "Well, surely, his name will be announced on the news tonight. Has Marylynn left the house?" "Yes, Miss Loren. We'll surely come and get you when the news comes on." "Thank you. I want you both to know that I don't blame you for what has happened today. It's not your fault. And don't worry. I'll take good care of him and we'll figure everything out in time. Okay? Now, you two should go get some rest." They nodded and left the room, closing the door behind them.

Once they were gone, I walked over to the sleeping child and studied his every feature. He was precious. Dark locks of wavy hair framed his round, cherubic face. His cheeks were full. He looked very healthy with chubby little arms and baby fat tucked beneath a cleft chin. He was obviously well cared for. Surely, there was a mom and dad out there frantically searching for him and wondering if they will ever see him alive again. Sadly, they would not be tucking him in to his bed tonight. I wanted to cry out loud at the thought. But now, I had this little boy to consider. I would need to be strong for him. "Lord, please help me", I whispered.

I quietly dressed into my pajamas and lay down next to the boy. I slipped under the covers and snuggled as close to him as I could. I was tired but didn't want to miss the nightly news. I knew they would be broadcasting this latest abduction. I needed sleep but didn't dare allow myself to even close my eyes. I would surely miss the news if I did. So, I turned out the light and just lay there listening to him breath. The sobbing had finally stopped and he seemed to be resting peacefully. Sleeping would be his only escape from reality from now on.

I watched the clock until just before 10:00 p.m.. I then slowly arose and walked into the bathroom. As quietly as I possibly could,

I tapped on the wall. Thad's bedroom was just on the other side of this wall. I heard nothing, so I tapped again. This time, in a loud whisper I said, "Thad...Thad...are you awake?" I heard him stirring around and then he said, "What?" "If Marylynn is gone can we watch the news?" "Yeh, she gone. Jis a minute Miss Loren." I heard the floor creak, then his door opened. He came and opened the door and immediately walked over to the sleeping child. He looked down at him with kindness but sadness in his eyes. He looked up at me. I could see he was feeling guilty. I said to him, "It's not your fault, Thad". He said, "C'mon Miss Loren. Lets go wake Ernie up. He won't mind at all." We left my room, leaving the door open in case the child should wake up, we would hear him. Ernie turned the television on and flipped to the news channel just in time to hear them announce the news was up next.

"Breaking news. Three months after the abduction of a young Riverside County girl, there is yet another missing child. This time a much younger child. Three year old Bradley Harris was playing at a nearby park when he suddenly disappeared. He was with his mother and his mother's friend at the time. Bradley had found some little friends to play with and had been running from one park toy to the other when the two women noticed he was no longer with the other children." A picture of Bradley appeared on the screen. I recognized him right away as being the little boy that now lay in my bed sleeping soundly. Such a beautiful child. My heart went out to his mother. His mother now appeared on the screen next to the photo of Bradley, crying and pleading for the return of her son. "He was there one minute and gone the next. I have no idea how he escaped my sight. We were talking and visiting but had been watching him play. He ran from the swings over to the slide. And then...he was just...gone." She burst into tears. Then, the announcer held the microphone up to Bradley's father. "Bradley is our pride and joy. He's our only child. He's a happy, healthy, perfect little guy. Keeps us entertained and laughing. He's a gift to us from God...our miracle child. We love him more than words could ever express. Please, please, whoever has him, please show some mercy and compassion and return our son to us. We will not press charges. We just want our son back." His chin quivering and fighting back tears. He stepped away from the microphone, turned his back on the reporter and walked over to his wife. They embraced in an outpouring of emotions.

The reporter then added that a search party had been formed to scour the surrounding area just in case, by some chance, the little boy had wandered off and was lost rather than abducted. There was a wooded area around the park and a mountain lion sighting had been reported a year or two ago. They were covering all bases. They would leave no stone unturned in the search for the missing child. Little did they know...

At the end of the broadcast, the case of the missing Ellis girl was mentioned. The reporter stated that at this point and time, there was no reason to believe the two cases were related in any way. They would keep the public informed of any new developments.

I thanked Ernie for allowing me to intrude on his sleep so I could watch the news. We now knew the little boy's name was Bradley. I hurried back to my room. Bradley was still sleeping peacefully. I slipped in under the covers and moved over near him. I had so many thoughts going through my head. How would I ever be able to care for him properly? I'd never had any siblings, much less younger ones. I had never babysat for little children. I'd never really spent any time around little kids at all. All I knew right now was that I was very tired and it was important for me to be rested. I had no idea what to expect come morning.

Morning arrived all too quickly and was accompanied by rain. I could hear the sound of rolling thunder off in the distance that seemed to be coming closer and closer with each lightning strike. The sky was dark and cloudy. The clouds were thick and ominous. The storm was far from over. The temperatures had been dipping into the low 40's lately and the feel of fall in the mountains was in the air. With the exception of the pines, trees were just beginning to show new color...orange, yellow, red. Fall would be in full swing very soon. Following fall would come winter. After winter...spring. I began to get way ahead of myself as my thoughts wandered.

I suddenly realized that the bed was damp. I rolled over to check on Bradley and he was awake, quietly looking up at me. He didn't move. He was afraid to move. He didn't know me and had no way of knowing if I was going to treat him unkindly as Marylynn had. His gaze switched from me to the ceiling. He had wet the bed and was gripped with fear. I said softly to him, "Good morning, Bradley. Don't be afraid. I won't hurt you. I will take care of you. Don't you worry, we'll find a way to get you home to Mommy, okay?" I wasn't sure how much he was comprehending but I was confident that speaking softly to him would bring him some measure of comfort and help him to be less afraid. His chin began to quiver and his eyes filled with tears. He didn't make one sound, however. He was trying so hard to be brave. I scooped him up into my arms and held him tightly. For the first time, he spoke very quietly. "I want Mommy". "I know you do. I promise to try and get you back to Mommy someday soon. But you'll have to be patient and very brave. It might take some time. Okay?" He didn't respond. I doubted that he was able to fully understand what I was saying. "I'm so sorry this has happened to you, Bradley. I'm going to need you to be a big boy and brave, like me, okay? No one is going to hurt you, Bradley. Here, let's go into the bathroom and get you out of these wet clothes, okay?" He nodded. I found a t-shirt for him to wear that would make do until we could get his clothes washed. He went along willingly and seemed more comfortable in the dry t-shirt. His feet were chubby and so short. But I put a pair of my clean socks on him along with his shoes to try and keep him warm. I removed all the wet bedding and threw it in the corner for Ernie and Thad to launder. Soon there were footsteps coming up the stairs. That meant breakfast was on the way. Good thing, too, because with everything going on last night, I'd had no dinner. I was very hungry. "Breakfast is on the way, Bradley. Are you hungry?" He shook his head, no. I figured once he saw and smelled the food, he would change his mind and eat something. The door opened. Bradley stiffened up when he saw Ernie and Thad. Not understanding the situation between them and Marylynn, he automatically assumed they were mean just like her. After all, they were the ones who physically captured him. As soon as they looked at him, his big, blue eyes got bigger and he shouted, "NO!"

Ernie spoke softly to Bradley. "We're so sorry little guy. We didn't want to do it." Thad, following after Ernie said, "Sorry, Bradley. We really are so sorry. We gonna try and make it up to ya, Buddy".

But as far as Bradley was concerned, these were the bad men that took him from his mother. They were the enemy. Unforgiving, he continued his glare and he slipped his chubby little arm through mine and held tight as though to prevent them from taking him again. He then ducked behind my arm so he wouldn't have to see them. I suggested that Thad and Ernie leave the platters of food in the room and come back later for them. I thought I may have better luck getting him to eat if the guys were not present. They readily agreed, grabbed the soiled laundry, and exited the room.

I began to remove lids off the platters to show Bradley what was available. Not knowing what Bradley liked, the guys had prepared a nice variety. "Look Bradley, scrambled eggs. Do you like scrambled eggs?" He shook his head, no. "Oh look at this, chocolate milk. Oooh...oatmeal. Cereal. Sausage, banana nut muffin, banana. I pointed at each item as I identified it. Yummy. Do you like bananas?" again, he shook his head, no. I assumed he would shake his head, no, at every suggestion. His appetite was likely not very good today. "Well, I thought all kids liked bananas. How about if we put this straw into this chocolate milk. It's fun to drink from a straw, right?" I put the straw up to his lips and he drank a couple swallows. I handed him a sausage link and he took it and bit into it. Success at last. He actually seemed to enjoy it so I offered another. He declined and didn't accept anything else. I was just satisfied that he'd eaten something. I proceeded to eat a little of most everything. It was tasty, especially after having had no dinner the night before.

Lightening cracked nearby. I knew the thunder was going to be loud and sudden. Sure enough...BOOM! Bradley jumped. His lower lip extended and began to quiver. The sound had scared him terribly. I scooted close to him, wrapped my arms around him and whispered, "It's only thunder. Just a noise, it can't hurt you." He leaned on me and seemed to accept my offer of comfort. That was a good sign.

## CHAPTER 13

# TRAGEDY STRIKES

· · · · · · · · · ·

D ays turned in to weeks. Weeks, into months. Winter had
arrived and was in full swing. The temperatures were frigid and
a blanket of snow changed the view entirely. It was beautiful
and an unusual sight for a Southern California flatlander girl.

Marylynn never gave Bradley any type of attention. Her only
acknowledgment of him was her occasional contribution of books,
puzzles, or items of clothing. It was clear she didn't care for males,
based on her treatment of not only Bradley, but Ernie and Thad as
well. Over the course of time, she had gotten to know and trust me,
at least to some degree. I had her convinced that I'd accepted my
situation and had come to look at her affectionately...like a mother.
She had taken me on a tour of the house and now allowed me and
Bradley, with special permission of course, to venture downstairs
and spend time in an outdoor courtyard. The small courtyard was
completely enclosed by a rock wall. There was a gate made of very
thick, rustic-looking wood, protected on both sides by heavy duty
padlocks. There was virtually no way of escape from that courtyard.
But, oftentimes, the beautiful German Shepherd, Princeton, would
be out there. Bradley and I had come to love him. He was gentle,
quiet, and very affectionate. His eyes showed kindness and he loved

being petted and spoken to. He seemed acutely aware of Bradley's small stature and took extra care to be gentle around him. This courtyard was the only outdoor area we were allowed to access. The courtyard in the front of the house was out of bounds and Marylynn made sure that fact was made clear to us. The rock wall was too high for me to see over. The wooden boards on the gate were tightly fitted together but there were a couple areas where the boards were slightly bent allowing for small cracks between them. Of course, I had to peek through just to find there was nothing but thick, dense, forest, on the other side.

Bradley had come to love and depend on me, and I on him as well. He truly was a little gift sent from Heaven and I thought about his parents often. He brought meaning to my life as it was now, and a reason to wake up everyday. He and I spent our days looking at pictures in magazines. I read stories to him daily. I colored in color books with him and we put together many puzzles. He was bright and smart and a very quick learner. My next goal would be teaching him to read. Oh, how I loved him. He fulfilled my desires to one day be a teacher. He was a perfect little subject and we made a great team, Bradley and I.

There was only one problem where Bradley was concerned. I found myself, almost daily, trying to devise a plan of escape, but with Bradley here, things would be far more complicated. No plan I could come up with seemed viable with little Bradley. Prayer was my only hope. And, I prayed often.

Then, one afternoon, I noticed Bradley was more quiet than usual. He had no appetite and turned down breakfast. He'd taken only a few sips of water. His forehead was warmer than usual. "Bradley," I asked, "are you feeling okay?" He shook his head, no. "I not few vewy good, Lowen". I dressed him back into his pajamas and put him into bed. I knew he had a fever so I covered him only with the sheet. I remembered what Mom did whenever I had a fever. I got a cloth wet with cool water and placed it on his forehead. "Lowen, will you wead me a stowie?" "Of course I will." I picked up a favorite book of his and began reading. Before I knew it, he had fallen asleep. Mom had always said that sleep was the best healer for children when they're sick. I kept a close eye on him and felt his forehead every hour. Nothing seemed to change. He remained warmer than usual. I didn't have a thermometer, so I had no idea how high his temperature was. It wouldn't have mattered anyway. I had no way of contacting Marylynn or a doctor, for that matter. All I could do was put more cool water on the cloth for his head. By that night, I noticed that his cheeks were very rosy and his head very hot. I rolled the sheet back and removed his pajama top. Now I was very concerned. I wasn't a doctor nor even an experienced mother and by now I'd run out of ideas on what I should do next. So, I prayed. "Oh God, please touch little Bradley and heal him. God, I don't know what to do and I need your help. Please." I began to cry.

Now, he was shivering. His fever was so high and I had removed his covers and pajama top. He opened his eyes and looked at me. "Lowen, my head huwts willy bad." Then I remembered my mother laying me down in a bathtub filled with tepid water. Oh, how I hated it. It felt like ice water when I was feverish.

"I'm so sorry you're sick, Bradley. Let's try one more thing. I'm going to put some water in the tub. You need to climb in and lay down in the water. It's going to feel very cold but it might help you to feel better. Okay?" He nodded yes and I went to fill the tub. He was a good sport. He trusted me and he climbed in to the tub. He slowly laid back until his body was in the water except for his head. He was shivering uncontrollably now. My heart broke, watching him go through this. He was such a sweet, trusting child. I kept him there for about five minutes but couldn't stand to see him suffer anymore. I helped him out of the tub and we put his pajama bottoms back on. I helped him to the bed and let him cover up with the sheet. His whole body was hot and rosy in color. He was covered in goose bumps and continued to shiver. I had him swallow a couple sips of water. He was so cooperative. I laid down next to him and took his hand in mine. "God, please touch Bradley and help him to be well". "Amen. Bradley followed with, "Amen". He drifted off to sleep. Eventually, so did I.

Morning came and I immediately reached for Bradley hoping that by now he might be feeling better. I felt his forehead and he felt much cooler...a bit too cool, in fact. I quickly sat up and looked down at Bradley. He lay motionless. His cheeks were no longer red. The color had left his face. I picked up his hand and it fell limp to the bed. He was not breathing. My heart dropped. NO...this cannot be. Please God, don't let it be. I shook him. "Bradley, wake up. C'mon...wake up. Don't leave me, Bradley." Bradley had passed away sometime in the night. I began to wail and beg God to bring him back to me. I grabbed him up and held him tightly. He was so cold now. "Why God, why? He was all I had. He was precious to me and now he will never be able to go home. Why did you take him"? For the first time in my life, I was angry with God...very angry. I laid Bradley back down on the bed and buried my face in my pillow and sobbed asking over and over again, "Why... why?" This was the last thing I expected. I had no idea Bradley was so ill.

There was a knock at the door. "Miss Loren, Miss Loren, is everything okay? The door opened and in stepped Ernie and Thad. I raised my head, my face wet with tears, and I looked at them. "Oh. Miss Loren, you been crying. We have your breakfast." Ernie said. "Oh Miss Loren. Why you cryin'?" Thad asked. At first I couldn't speak. "Bradley is gone." "Whattaya mean, Miss Loren. Bradley is layin right there next to you. He ain't gone, Miss Loren." "No Ernie, Bradley passed away in his sleep last night. He's dead. He was sick last night. I tried to take care of him but it didn't work. He must have been sicker than I thought. I had no medicine for him...no doctor. He didn't make it." "Oh my goodness, Miss Loren. What we gonna do"? They both began to cry. We sorry, Miss Loren. We know how much he meant to you. We loved him, too." "I know you did. You both helped me take very good care of him. And he had grown to love both of you, too." I looked at Ernie and asked, "Do you happen to know when Marylynn is expected to be home?" "I think she said she would be home tonight." "Okay. You guys can leave a little something here for me to eat. I may eat it later. Right now, I would like to spend a little time alone with Bradley, if you don't mind". "No problem, Miss Loren. We understand. Just ring the bell if you need us for anything." I nodded, and they left the room.

I had to pull myself together and force myself to be strong again. There was a much bigger picture that I could not allow myself to lose sight of. I walked around the bed to where Bradley lay. How will I ever be able to face his parents with what has happened to him? What incredibly sad news this will be for them. I looked down at his sweet, cherubic face. He looked so peaceful. Even in death he was a beautiful boy. I was lost in my loneliness. Oh, how I will miss you. Heaven has gained such a precious jewel today. I could no longer hold back tears. I'd just have be strong later because I couldn't do it right then. As the tears flowed down my face, I pulled the sheet back and laid it alongside of him. I gently rolled his body toward me and slipped the sheet underneath him. Then, I rolled his body onto the sheet until he was completely wrapped. I opened the closet door and laid his pillow on the floor toward the back of the closet. I picked up his body and carried him into the closet and laid him down placing his head gently on the pillow. Oh, how hard it was for me to walk out of the closet leaving him in there alone and then to close the door behind me. I looked around the room. All the evidence of his life remained. The books that he loved to have me read to him still lay on the desk next to all the little pictures we colored together. A partially constructed puzzle that he got tired of working on. He planned to help me finish it tomorrow. The room was so quiet. How will my life go on without him? The reality of losing Bradley was hitting me hard, like an arrow to the heart. I cried out loud, like a baby would. I didn't care if anyone heard me. I could not help myself. The enormous loss might be more than I can ever handle. I don't believe I will ever recover. Life can be so cruel. "Oh God, after everything else...why this?"

I wished there was a way to get him home to his parents so they could give him a proper burial. I wondered how Marylynn was going to handle this situation. What would she do with his body? She didn't love him at all. He should be going home to his parents. I glanced over at the closet door. I didn't want Marylynn touching his body. I didn't want her to even look at him. I said a little prayer.

"Oh God in Heaven. I know you are holding Bradley in your loving arms right now. How I wish he were in mine. I don't understand your ways. You know how broken I am right now. Please give me the strength I'm going to need in the days ahead. Thank you for the time you gave with Bradley, to know and to love him. And please, say "hello" to him for me and tell him thank you for being such a special and treasured friend to me. Tell him I miss him terribly but I know he is in good hands and he is no longer ill. Goodbye Bradley. I'm going to miss you more than words can ever say. Amen."

Now there was nothing more I could do but wait for Marylynn to come home. I lay on the bed lost in thoughts. I had no appetite at all. Ernie and Thad checked on me several times asking if there was anything they could do for me or if I was hungry. There was nothing they could do. Everything I needed was completely out of their realm of abilities to help me with.

The sun was going down now and Marylynn still was not home. Just then, I heard the gate open. I felt a chill go up my spine. I sat and waited knowing that Ernie and Thad would break the news to her as soon as she came in to the house. Sure enough...footsteps coming up the stairs. The door opened and there she stood. "Oh my dear little Loren. What has happened?" I just looked at her. I knew that she was fully aware of what had happened. I felt like the information was far too sacred to share with such a shallow, disdainful, woman. So I offered no words. "Loren", she asked in a more serious tone, "I asked you what happened." If I was to remain in her good graces I knew I'd better speak up. "Bradley became ill yesterday. He had a very high fever. I did what I could but it wasn't enough. He passed away in his sleep sometime during the night." I was now feeling intense sorrow mixed with extreme anger. I hoped she would assume my behavior was born only in sorrow. She didn't know me well enough to decipher this unusual behavior in me. I'd never shown her my anger. I was glad of that. I wanted to blame her...to tell her that Bradley had needed a doctor and had I been able to get proper help for him he might be alive right now. But at this time, there was nothing that could be done to help Bradley so I had to hold my tongue and remember that I still needed to make it out of here alive. So, DON'T MAKE MARYLYNN ANGRY! I would have to remind myself of this everyday.

"Where is he?", she asked. "I laid him in the closet. He's wrapped in a sheet." She immediately walked to the closet and opened the door. She gazed into the closet then closed the door and rang the bell to summon Ernie and Thad. They came running and appeared at the bedroom door. "Come get this out of here. I'll give you instructions downstairs." Ernie hurried to the closet, scooped up Bradley's body and without looking at me, he disappeared out of the bedroom. "I'll have Ernest and Thaddeus take care of this situation. I'm sorry you lost your brother. I know you cared very much for him and he was in good hands with you. So try not to take it to heart and don't blame yourself. Sometimes life just happens. We can't possibly understand everything in life." She turned and left the room. I was in awe of her total lack of understanding, compassion, and depth of character. She was like the shell of a human with nothing of substance on the inside. The things she had just said to me was her best effort at offering words of comfort. I was dumbfounded...but not surprised.

I wondered what she had in mind to do with the body. I would pretend to go to bed early so I could have my bedroom lamp off and watch out the window undetected. I knew she was too smart to bury him on the property. I dressed into pajamas then switched off the lamp. I stood at the window, waiting. Sure enough, after just a few minutes, the engine to the van started up. I saw it pulling out of the driveway, only this time, it was pulling a small row boat on a trailer attached to the back. Oh no. They're going to weight his body down and drop him into the lake. I knew that Bradley wouldn't know the difference, he wouldn't feel anything but to me, it was horrible. To Marylynn, he had no more value than an old tire or an empty soda can. They disappeared down the long driveway with my precious Bradley and I knew where they were going.

I laid down and waited for them to return. It was well over two hours before I heard them coming up the driveway. I just stayed where I lay, knowing that little Bradley was now lying at the bottom of the cold, murky lake. Oh yes, I was filing away mental notes that I was surely going to need in the future. Marylynn's day was coming. Be patient, Timmie...be patient, and be smart. Keep your head, Girl, if you ever want to see justice done.

As I lay there in the dark, I heard footsteps coming up the stairs. Thad had gone into his room and shut the door behind him. I heard him sobbing. My heart went out to these two unfortunate men who hadn't the mental capacity to see their way out of their situation. They were trapped and forced into taking part in activities that were completely opposed to their own innocent characters. One day I would be in a position to help them as well.

CHAPTER 14

# THE PROMISE

. . . . . . . . . .

T he days following the death of Bradley seemed surreal. The quiet was deafening. It didn't help that the weather was cold and the sky remained gray all day. I was in a state of depression that gave no signs of ever letting up. All I wanted to do was stay in my pajamas and curl up in bed. I was glad that Marylynn was once again out of town. She would likely not allow my emotional state to manifest itself in such a way. But, I needed this time to be alone in utter seclusion from the world. I was in mourning and it didn't seem to me to be out of the question to be experiencing such mental agony. After all, Marylynn was responsible for my life of seclusion even without the loss of Bradley. For a moment, anger took the forefront of my emotions. Ernie and Thad were the only things that kept me tied to the real world...that forced me to deal with the fact that I couldn't remain in this state of mind forever. I still had to eat occasionally. They reminded me to shower and brush my teeth. I probably would not have, otherwise. I didn't like them bothering me but I'm glad they did.

Oh, how I missed the cheerfulness, the innocent laughter, the cute and childish conversations I had with Bradley. He was such a bright and shining little star in a world of ugliness and chaos.

No wonder God took him His presence gave me a reason to keep
going, to keep hoping, and a determination to make our way home,
eventually.

I needed a reason to get out of bed but there was nothing I could
think of that I wanted to do. So I began taking Bradley's clothes
out of the chest of drawers, folding and re-folding them and putting
them away. I looked at the pictures he'd colored and colored the
picture on the opposite page. I read the books out loud that I had
read to him. Doing these things brought me as close to him as I
was ever going get. Finally, I progressed to a point where I could no
longer bear to see his things. I placed everything... his little brown
shoes, all his clothes, books, crayons...everything, in the bottom
drawer and determined not to open it again until the time came
when I could hand it all over to his parents.

A few nights later, it snowed. The blanket of white that covered
the ground and the sparkly limbs of the trees were so beautiful the
next morning. It looked like God had sprinkled powdered sugar
over the whole world. The sight would have thrilled Bradley. What
a lovely painting it would have made. It looked like a postcard. I had
to crack open the window to feel the air. A frigid breeze stung my
cheeks so I quickly shut the window as thoughts of Bradley came
flooding in and darkness enveloped my mind once again. I buried
my face in the pillow and cried til I thought I would have no tears
left. I promised Bradley that one day soon, Marylynn would pay for
what she did to him. I knew he was with God and that he was okay
though the thought of him lying at the bottom of the lake tormented
me relentlessly.

I woke up to sunshine beaming through my window. I had lost
all track of time and wasn't sure if this was the same day or if it was
the next. I suppose under the circumstances, it didn't really matter.
The sunshine had brought with it a new attitude, a new insight,
and reminder that life had to go on, whether I wanted it to or not.
I couldn't stay in this state of mourning forever. I needed to pull
myself up and move forward. I wanted to go home.

CHAPTER 15

# PLANS IN THE MAKING

· · · · · · · · · ·

E rnie had begun making a habit of allowing me into his room to watch the nightly news whenever Marylynn was not at home, even if there was going to be no mention of the Ellis case. Tonight was no exception. Interestingly, the news began with an update on the recent child abductions. Detective Shore was handed the microphone and he began speaking with the usual confidence he'd always exhibited. "We have every reason to believe after extensive investigations that the two missing children are not only still alive but that they were abducted by the same individual or individuals. We are getting ever closer to breaking this case. The day is coming when the perpetrator is going to make a mistake. And when that happens, I will be right there breathing down their neck." He looked straight into the camera and continued. "If the responsible party is watching right now, I want you to know that we are closing in and your days are numbered. You will pay for your crimes." He smiled, clicked his tongue and winked.

I had to smile. He was amusing. I was betting that he was playing psychological games with whomever the guilty party was.

But it was apparent he'd come across some kind of evidence linking the two abductions. He was right. Unfortunately, he was wrong about one thing...little Bradley was no longer alive.

I could only imagine how Marylynn was taking Shore's updates. He was likely causing her some degree of anxiety, wondering if he really was closing in on her or if he was just playing "cop" games. I'll bet she hated him, nonetheless. I glanced over at Ernie and noticed he was crying. "What's wrong, Ernie?" "If that cop finds us, me and Thad will go to jail for the rest of our whole life." "Oh no, Ernie," placing my hand on his shoulder. "Don't you worry about that. If it ever happens that the cop finds out about you guys and Marylynn, I will be sure to tell him that you and Thad didn't want to do any of it. I'll tell him that Marylynn made you do it. I'll tell him Marylynn threatened to hurt you real bad if you didn't do what she said. I promise you will not be in trouble. You need to trust me. I would never let you guys take blame for this. You both have been so good to me and I care very much about you. Okay?" "Okay, Miss Loren. Thank you, Miss Loren. We love you." Then Thad added, "Yeh, we love you, Miss Loren."

What Ernie and Thad began discussing next really grabbed my attention. "Guess what, Miss Loren.

My Aunt Melba is coming in two more days to pick me and Ernie up to take us down the hill for the day." "Really? That sounds like fun." "It is. Marylynn lets her pick us up once a year to visit for the day." "You only get to see her once a year?" "Yes. If I wanna keep livin' here, I have to stick to the rules." "I see." "And, Miss Marylynn's rules are that Ernie has to be allowed to go along with us... which makes it way more fun for me, anyway. Plus, Aunt Melba likes Ernie and wants him to go with us even if it wasn't a rule. And, the second rule is, Aunt Melba is not allowed to come into the house. Especially now, with you bein' here, Miss Loren. But we can't tell her why she ain't allowed in."

My mind immediately went into planning mode. How could I use this new development to my own advantage? I hated to think this way. I didn't like the idea of using Ernie and Thad to further my own agenda. But, my resources were limited, after all. I had to seize every opportunity available. So..."Where do you guys go when she picks you up. What kind of stuff do you guys do?"

They were both so excited they began to speak all at once. I couldn't understand a word they said. "Whoa, whoa...I can't hear when both of you talk. One at a time, please." They laughed. "Why don't we let Thad go first since it's his aunt." They agreed. "Well, first she takes us to a restaurant for something to eat. Then, she takes us to a five and dime store and gives us money to buy stuff." "What kind of things do you like to buy?" "Well, we like crayons and color books because that's something we can do together. Once, we bought a game of checkers, which we still have and we play sometimes." Ernie cut in and added that if they have time after that, sometimes they get to go to a movie or go skating. And always, before they go home, Aunt Melba stops for ice cream cones.

She sounded like an exceptional lady who truly cared about these two guys. Surely, she must have caught on to the fact that Marylynn is an anti-social, hateful woman, who has something to hide. No doubt, she must be very curious about what it is.

Ernie continued, "She is always so nice to us. When we go to the movies she always buys us candy, like Good-n-Plenty, Milk Duds, popcorn, Bon-bons, that's my favorite, and soda. Our favorite part of every movie is the cartoons at the very beginning. I love the movies but my favorite part of the whole day is when she takes us to the five and dime store and I can pick whatever I want." Then Thad added, "and plus, she takes us for a drive past our old school where me and Ernie first became friends. I wish we could see our old teacher. She was the nicest teacher ever."

His comment gave me pause to think back on my own teacher, Miss Turner. What a wonderful lady and mentor she was. Such a great example of compassion, respect, and encouragement. I hope to see her again, as well.

"Can you think of something you'd like for us to pick up for you at the five and dime, Miss Loren?"

"It's so nice of you to ask, Thad. Let me think for minute." My mind immediately went to what I may be able to use when I make a break for it one of these days.

"Well, a flashlight would be nice so I can find my way to the bathroom at night without having to turn on the lamp. Or, even a little compass. I always wanted to learn how to use one just for fun. Also, a journal would be nice so I can write poems, along with a couple of writing pens in case one pen runs out of ink." "We sure will look for those things, Miss Loren." "If you can't find them, it's okay. I just want you guys to have a good time. So don't worry about it, okay?"

I was thinking to myself that these items may really turn out to be necessities. My dad had taught me how to use a compass one summer when we went to the mountains on a camping trip. He said, "Now you keep this in your pocket the entire time we're here. You know how to use it in case you should get lost. But the best medicine is prevention. Don't go walking off on your own...ever."

At this point in time, I had no idea what the future held. I did know that if I were ever to find my way out of this house, I would need help navigating these forests and a compass may be my only guide. I hoped I could still remember how to use one. The forests are so thick in some areas that at night it's utter darkness without some sort of light source. I was definitely not looking forward to facing the forest alone, especially at night. The very thought struck a certain fear in me and I realized, I dared not dwell on it. For if I thought about it for too long, I may never leave this house.

Feeling tired, but with a renewed hope, I bid my friends a goodnight and they walked me to my room. Ernie locked the bedroom door behind me just as the screech of the gate could be heard. I put my face close to the door and said, "Guys, I hear the gate. Hurry and get to your rooms." I heard them scramble to their rooms and each door quietly shut behind them. Close call, for sure. I didn't turn my lamp on. I just jumped into bed and pulled the covers up. It was much later than what we were accustomed to being in bed but we had had a very nice visit. The evening news had been especially enlightening. And I had gained a bit more ground on formulating a plan. I would just take it a day at a time. I felt that God was leading me and I needed to trust him and be patient.

The next morning, fully aware that Marylynn was home, I wondered what her plans were. I was hungry but it was only 7:00. Breakfast would be served in about an hour. Would she be ordering her breakfast to be served in my room? I decided to roll out of bed, shower and get prepared for that possibility. I was glad that I'd had time to work through some of my depression and mourning over Bradley. I knew there would be good days and bad days but today, I was in a planning-for-my-future mode and was ready to begin facing the inevitable.

Eight o'clock sharp brought the sound of footsteps up the stairs and to my room. The door swung open and Ernie stood there alone, no trays in hand. "Miss Loren," he said, "Miss Marylynn has requested the honor of your presence to join her in her private dining room for breakfast." I was taken aback. This was the last thing I had expected, but I was also delighted. And I was very glad that I had cleaned up and was prepared to join her. This was perfect. I was exhilarated and at the same time, felt a degree of dread. One never knew what kind of mood Marylynn was apt to be in. This was one more positive sign that Marylynn was accepting me more and more and maybe even beginning to trust me. Still, it was nearly impossible to put my guard down and just enjoy breakfast. I had to always be aware of my manners, and keep in mind her critical eye knowing she was always at the ready to correct others for the slightest infraction. Sharing breakfast with her was more than unsettling. I didn't like having to pretend I liked her, especially since my true feelings for her were that of pure loathing. I forced myself not to think about it. I was afraid the truth might shine through.

"Well Ernest, I'll be glad to join Mother for breakfast", as I grinned at him and he shot me a grin right back. I followed as he descended the stairwell and proceeded toward the formal dining room. The closer we came to our final destination, the more nervous I became. *Calm down, Timmie.* I reasoned with myself. My heart was pumping a little faster and my breaths had become shorter and a bit shallower, as usual. I paused for a moment just before rounding the corner into the dining room, and took in a deep breath then slowly let it out. I continued around the corner where Marylynn sat stoically at the head of the massive dining table. There before her set a cup of tea and a bagel on a saucer. It seemed a bit humorous and a waste of such a large table to have but a minute morsel set there on the edge. I withheld a chuckle. Thad pulled back a chair and motioned for me to be seated. After I sat, he scooted the chair nearer the table then disappeared around the corner to the kitchen. In just a moment he reappeared with a tray that he set on the table before me. He removed the lid to reveal my breakfast which far exceeded the minuscule amount Marylynn was having for breakfast. I felt gluttonous knowing I could easily consume the amount set before me. And now she would be watching me. I thanked Ernest and proceeded to open the napkin, placing it on my lap. There was a short-lived but awkward moment of silence. Then, without lifting her eyes to look at me, she said in a quiet voice, quite untypical of herself, "Good morning, Loren." I responded, "Good morning, Mother."

She noticed my glancing at her breakfast and then back at my own. She must have known what I was thinking because she said, "Don't worry about what I'm eating. You're very small so it's important that you get enough to eat. Your growing body requires more nutrition. Eat your breakfast while it's still hot." Her words did put my mind at some ease as I was concerned that enjoying a full breakfast was going to make me look like a pig. "Yes Mother, you're right." I began eating, taking small, deliberate bites, carefully chewing each bite and using my napkin to dab my lips occasionally which I made sure to keep closed while chewing.

Marylynn, now gazing at me straight-on asked, "Loren, how have you been doing lately...I mean, are you doing okay since losing Bradley?" Oh how I wish she hadn't asked. Immediately, I wanted to cry. I felt my chin begin to quiver and my eyes furrowed with no help from me. I took a deep breath before speaking and let it out slowly. "Well, to be honest, it has been difficult for me lately, but I'm trying hard to move forward without him. He will be deeply missed. He had become very special to me." I took another bite of food and did not look at her. Marylynn adjusted herself in her chair as though she wasn't sure what to say next.

"I've been reading more of the books you got for me. Some have turned out to be quite interesting, worthwhile reading. Also, I've been exercising some...anything I can think of to fill the hours. I hope to look as fit and trim as you do when I'm an adult." This comment seemed to please her. A hint of a smile showed on her face.

"I'm sorry I've been absent from the house so much lately. Circumstances have deemed it impossible for me to be home more. I'm hoping that this trend will change soon. We should spend more time together, you and me." I wasn't sure I liked the idea but I responded as I should. "That would be wonderful, Mother. I'd like that a lot." "I will be leaving later this afternoon but will return home late tonight. I will be spending the entire day with you tomorrow as Ernest and Thaddeus will be gone. Thaddeus' aunt picks them up on occasion and takes them for outings. So, it will be just you and myself for the entire day. I have instructed Ernest and Thaddeus to take you on a tour of the kitchen so you'll know your way around when it comes time to prepare meals for the two of us. They will acquaint you with the menu and everything will be prepared in advance and will only need to be heated. You and I can spend the day getting to know each other better." "That sounds like a capital idea, Mother". *I hoped I didn't sound like I was trying too hard to sound sophisticated.* "I haven't cooked for a long time and I actually miss being in the kitchen."

I suddenly noticed I had eaten nearly all the breakfast and I was quite full. Marylynn scooted her chair away from the table and stood up. "Ernest, you may clear the dishes from the table and then show Loren around the kitchen as I instructed earlier. But first, I want to speak with you and Thaddeus, alone." I took that as my cue to wander away from the immediate area and head toward the kitchen. Thad stood before the open refrigerator carefully placing food items in their designated areas. As I entered, he turned, startled at first that it was I who appeared in the doorway rather than the usual, Ernie. I relayed Marylynn's request to speak with he and Ernie alone. Without a word, he shut the refrigerator door and headed toward the dining room. I continued to wander the kitchen. I could hear muffled conversation coming from the dining room but couldn't decipher the words. I looked over at the kitchen door. The same door they had brought me through when I first arrived. How easy it would be to run out that door. But I knew that once I got outside, I wouldn't have the slightest idea of how to get off of the property and they would catch me for sure. Marylynn would know she would never be able to trust me and I would likely end up at the bottom of the lake. So, not a good idea. Patience. This was the only solution to the problem...and something that I was never good at.

Now, I was hearing Ernie and Thad answering, "Yes ma'am" after each command, and then her final command..."and I mean every word. You two slip up and say one word about any of this and I will surely know. You will pay with your lives. I will tell them that you both did it all yourselves. They will believe me, not you. You will go to jail forever. Do not forget!" "No ma'am, we won't forget. Promise". Both men were thoroughly frightened and assuring Marylynn that she had nothing to worry about as they promised to keep their mouths shut about me and Bradley. She was a horrible woman. Detective Shore was right. She was surely going to pay for her crimes one day. What a day that will be.

Meanwhile, I was amazed and pleased with the freedom I was enjoying just wandering the kitchen alone. I had definitely gained some serious progress. It was all about taking little steps. I was careful to not give Marylynn cause to doubt me.

Soon after overhearing Marylynn's demands to the boys, they appeared at the kitchen door. Both looking a bit pale and shaken but trying their best to put on a smile. This was their true nature. They were careful to behave as though we were unfamiliar as friends. Our only connection with each other was as Marylynn's daughter versus "the help". They showed me where everything was kept. The silverware drawer. Plates, glasses, other utensils. Then they opened the refrigerator door and showed me what Marylynn and I would be having for breakfast the next morning and what needed to be done to prepare it. I would only need the microwave to heat the food. Then they progressed on to show what would be for lunch and then dinner. They also showed me where snacks were kept and what was available if I wanted to take some of them up to my room...which I did. I was thinking that I could start a little stockpile of goodies to take with me on a journey I'd be making one day in the near future. Once they'd shown me everything, it was time for me to retreat to my room with my bag of goodies in tow. I suspected that Marylynn was lurking around a corner somewhere listening and observing the relationship between me and the guys. She needed continual confirmation that her orders for us to remain strangers, in a sense, were being met and obeyed.

Sure enough, just as we were approaching the stairway, a pair of double doors slowly opened and Marylynn appeared. "Ernest, bring Loren into the library." She turned and disappeared into the room. "Yes Ma'am. Come this way, Miss Loren." We walked toward the huge double doors and entered a large room full of elaborate, dark wood shelves filled with books. I had never seen so many books. There was a fireplace burning brightly and the warmth from it could be felt several feet away. It cracked and popped and made the large room seem cozy. I wanted to sit near it but Marylynn beckoned me to come sit at the desk near her. I obediently sat on the available chair. "You enjoy reading, don't you, Loren?" "Yes, I do, Mother."

"This library contains a large number of volumes though they are not likely suited to your interests. My late father was not only a student of law, but was also a renowned architect. These books were his collection...each and every one read by him in its entirety, many of them more than once." I raised my eyebrows to show I was in awe. She continued, "I always admired my father's superior intellect. He was in perpetual pursuit of knowledge. This very room was where he did his reading and studying. This was his office, his library, his classroom, of sorts. When he wasn't studying, he was teaching others what he knew on any one of these varied subjects. He mastered anything and everything he set his mind to learn. A brilliant man, he was, and I miss him. I feel near him when I'm in this room." This was the first time I'd seen any semblance of warmth and compassion in Marylynn. I believed she truly did miss him.

She took a deep breath and raised her chin as though preparing to begin a new subject, which is exactly what she did. "Enough about my father, let's talk about you. Tell be more about your interests."

"Well, I enjoy painting though I'm not very good at it. I enjoy art. Someday, I would like to write a book. I would be interested in training canines to become seeing eye dogs or even for police work."

"Well, that's fascinating!" She seemed truly impressed. "Let's see if we can do something to facilitate that interest. Yes, we'll see what we can do. You've met Princeton, have you not?" "Yes, Mother. He's an amazing dog. So beautiful and friendly. His name fits him well." "I'll do some research and see what books are available for training. This would give you something to do and Princeton would surely love the extra attention." "Oh, what a wonderful idea. Yes, I would like that." This is exactly what I was hoping for. I could get to know Princeton well, train him, and take him with me when I go. "Wonderful," she replied. "Tomorrow, when Ernest and Thaddeus are gone, you and I can take a stroll around the property and Princeton can tag along. You can become better acquainted with him and with me as well. I think you'll be impressed with the property. The snow has melted off a bit so I think the paths will be visible. It's a lovely walk." She was definitely loosening up. She had a friendly and personable side to her but I was fully aware of how quickly that could change. I couldn't let my guard down even for a moment, unless I wanted to risk ending up at the bottom of the lake.

I sensed our visit was about to end. She rose from her chair and said, "You will need to dress warmly. The air outdoors is quite frigid." I assured her that I would. It was clear that Marylynn was highly intelligent. She was also insane. "I'm going to enjoy having you as a daughter," she commented.

## CHAPTER 16

# STROLLING WITH MARYLYNN

. . . . . . . . . .

I slept soundly and was not at all ready for the knock that came to my door at 7:00 a.m.. It was Ernie, tapping lightly on my door. "Miss Loren...Miss Loren, are you awake?" "Yes Ernie. C'mon in." He opened the door and asked as pleasantly and quietly as he could, "Miss Loren, do you remember you're making breakfast for you and Miss Marylynn?" "Oh, goodness, yes. I suppose I should have set my alarm. Thank you for reminding me." "Miss Loren, Marylynn told me to tell you to stay away from the window when Aunt Melba arrives. So when you hear the gate..." "What time is she arriving?" "I'm not sure but she said it would be early. You should wait to go downstairs and serve breakfast until she has left with me and Thad. Marylynn says she don't need anyone snoopin' around askin' questions about who is that up in the window." "Don't worry, Ernie. I'll stay away from the window."

So, in the meantime, I got dressed and waited for Aunt Melba to arrive. But if Marylynn thinks I'm not going to be looking out the window, she can think again. I walked over to the window curtains and arranged them so there would be a crack in the curtains that would allow me to see out but no one would be able to see me.

"Thank you, Miss Loren." Then he leaned toward me and whispered, "We're gonna miss you today. And don't worry. We won't forget to look for the stuff you asked for. But you have to always keep it hid real good from Marylynn. If she ever sees you with stuff that she didn't buy, me and Thad will be in big trouble." "You have my word, Ernie. She'll never see any of it. You and Thad just worry about having a good time today, okay?" "Okay Miss Loren," he said with a smile.

Just then, the screech of the gate interrupted our final goodbyes. A look of surprise and elation appeared on Ernie's face. He quickly gave me a floppy-handed wave and shut the door, ran to his room to grab his backpack full of stuff he'd likely not need then ran down stairs. I heard him tell Thad to hurry up because he'd heard the gate. Thad responded, "I know, I heard it too. I'm comin'."

I ambled over to the window curtain, careful to stay hidden, and watched the driveway until I saw a black sedan rolling up to the front of the home. It came to a stop and immediately the driver's door opened. An elderly black woman climbed out, stood up, and stretched a little. It had been a long drive. But she had no need to approach the front door as it swung open and Thad and Ernie rushed out to meet her. Despite the chilly temperatures, the lady was wearing a mid-shin length silky dress, a sweater with a muffler around her neck and a pair of gloves. A pleasant looking woman who, upon seeing the guys running toward her, broke out in a huge open-mouthed grin. I could hear her elation as she let out a loud squeal, "Ohhhh, here comes my favorite guys in the whole world. I have missed you so much". She grabbed them with vigor and hugged them both tightly. They hugged her back as they laughed and hugged some more. I had never seen them this gleeful before and the sight made me smile. The laughing and celebrating suddenly halted as Marylynn approached the group. I couldn't hear what she was saying. Most likely asking when they would be expected back home, etc. I noticed Marylynn take a quick sideways glance up at my window. I knew she could not see me hidden so strategically. She looked away and continued her dialogue with Aunt Melba. In a moment, the guys climbed into the vehicle. Thad sat in the front passenger seat and Ernie took the back. Aunt Melba checked their doors for safety as Marylynn turned to go into the house. As Melba opened her own door to climb in, she took a quick glance up at the house. I knew I shouldn't but I moved the curtain just enough that I knew she saw it. She took a double-take and glanced up again. I knew she had seen the curtain move but I hoped she'd not mention it right away. I continued to watch until the vehicle was out of sight and out the gate.

I knew Marylynn would be on her way to my room any moment now. So, I readied myself near the door. I grabbed my coat, knit cap and gloves. I was ready for the walk we'd be taking after breakfast. She approached my room and said cheerfully, "Good morning, Loren. I trust you are feeling well this morning and are ready for our after-breakfast stroll?" She spoke to me as though we'd known each other all our lives and were the very best of friends. She lived in a world of fantasy. But I went along with it (as any good daughter should) and replied, "Yes, Mother. I've been anxiously waiting for our stroll today. I'll go to the kitchen and grab our breakfast." She smiled and agreed. I prepared everything as Ernie had shown me and we enjoyed a breakfast at the dinette table in the kitchen, much less formal than in the large dining room as before. I think this was where Ernie and Thad were used to eating. She really seemed to be letting her hair down today...trying to relax and have a good time. It was so out of character for her.

We ate and chatted. Just small talk. Had I not known better, I'd have thought I was with a normal person, someone likable and friendly. I almost forgot how much I loathed her. If this were the beginning of a new trend, my get-away may turn out to be much easier for me than I ever imagined. As soon as we finished eating, I gathered up the dishes, took them to the kitchen as though I was accustomed to doing so, and placed them into the dishwasher. I think she was enjoying how comfortable I appeared to be in my new surroundings. She said, "Oh, I *am* going to enjoy being a mother. It's wonderful having you here." "Well, thank you, Mother. I feel the same. I feel as though I've always known you."

"Well, are we ready to venture out?" she asked. "Absolutely" I said as I began to put on my coat, hat, and gloves. "I'm ready." I answered with a grin.

We headed toward the front door. She pushed some buttons on a wall switch to disable what I assumed to be a house alarm. As she opened the door, Princeton loped up to us and sat on the porch waiting to be petted. "Well, good morning, Princeton," She said. "So nice to see you. Now say hello to Miss Loren." I petted his head and scratched behind his ears and said good morning to him. He enjoyed the attention and seemed willing to sit there just as long as I was willing to keep petting him. Then I added, "Guess what, Princeton, Mother is going to get a special book for me so I can learn how to train you to do things. I think we'll make good friends, you and me. Does that sound like fun, Princeton?" He wagged his tail and stood up. His tongue hung out as he panted a bit and looked up at me. He had such kind eyes. "I think he'll like me alright. I'm going to enjoy the challenge." I was thinking of what a valued friend he was going to become.

"Princeton is a good dog...if you like dogs. Personally, I don't particularly like how they smell or how they shed. I have to wash my hands immediately if I pet them. The only reason I keep him is because he was my father's dog. My father loved him very much... and I loved my father."

Oh, how I wanted to ask questions about her father, how long had he been gone. I wanted to ask about her mother and I wondered if she would ever divulge the fact that she had had a sister.

"Anyway," she continued, "Ernest and Thaddeus don't give him much attention which is another reason I think your spending time training him would be a very good thing...for him and for you."

"Let's walk" she said as she stepped off the porch. "You haven't seen the grounds yet, have you?" "No, I sure haven't." She knew very well I hadn't. "I've seen only what is visible from my bedroom window. This courtyard is lovely. I noticed that the painting in my room is of this very courtyard. I'm curious who painted it." I hoped I wasn't walking on dangerous grounds. I had assumed it was the younger sister who had painted the scene. Marylynn stiffened a bit but in a quiet voice she said, "That picture was painted by my younger sister who is no longer with us. She passed away shortly after my father did." She quickly changed the subject. Over in this area is where my mother used to plant her flower garden. In the spring, all the lovely bulbs grow shoots that produce the most beautiful, colorful array of flowers. She had quite the green thumb. All these trees lining the walk-way were planted by her as well. She designed and had the arbors built to her liking. She had an excellent eye for landscaping but not too much else. She was quite domestic in her attitudes and thinking. No career interests to speak of. Any spare time she had was spent with my sister...my sweet, dear, little sister." I noticed a distinct tone of sarcasm. I had to assume there had been a history of jealousy over the extra attention her younger sister had been given because of her illness. Also, it was obvious she had no respect for the fact that her mother had no interest in pursuing some form of career but rather was a domestic woman by nature, happy to be at home taking care of her children and the gardening. She spoke with utter disdain in her voice and it showed also in her expressions whenever the subject of her mother was brought up. Apparently, following the death of her father, she had seen no benefit in keeping her mother or her sister around. Ernie, on the other hand, would come in quite handy as free labor and helping in certain situations when needed. I wondered how many bodies might eventually be discovered at the bottom of the lake.

I set my thoughts aside in order to make conversation with Marylynn. "Even in mid-winter this property is amazing. I can only imagine how lovely it is in the spring and summer once the snow is all gone." "Yes, it is very lovely, indeed. All the colors of the rainbow adorn this courtyard all the way down the driveway to the road and to the back of the property. Ernest and Thaddeus are the groundskeepers. They do a pretty decent job of keeping it in order." I could hardly believe she gave them credit for a job well done. I wondered if she ever told them?

As we walked, I let Marylynn carry the conversation whenever possible so I could survey the surroundings with less interruption. Soon, the snow would be melting and the air would be more pleasant, at least during daylight hours.

Marylynn seemed to be feeling more comfortable with me by the minute. She jabbered on about the different types of trees and shrubbery that would appear once the weather warmed. She was excited for spring to arrive.

I noticed the entire property was fenced. Parts of it were fenced in block wall topped with decorative wrought iron. This was mainly in the front areas of the property and was for street appeal, mostly. But towards the back of the property, some areas were fenced in wood while others were protected by chain link. The chain link gave better support for vines and climbing plants such as berries, sweet peas, etc as Marylynn explained. For now, all the vines were dormant. Then, there it was. Nestled down at the very bottom of the chain link fencing and partially hidden by shrubs, appeared the perfect escape route. Thick forest surrounded the property and Princeton had apparently dug a generous gap under the chain link in order to escape into the woods to explore. The dugout was conveniently camouflaged by icy, leafless brush and shrubbery. I made sure to not keep my eyes on the area as I did not want Marylynn to notice and look over to see what I was looking at. I quickly averted my attention but kept mental notes so as not to forget exactly where the spot was located. I smiled to myself. God bless that dog.

Suddenly, I realized Marylynn had asked me a question. I had been so caught up in my new discovery that I had allowed my attention to be interrupted from her rambling. This is just what I was afraid would happen. She was looking at me with annoyance in her eyes as she waited for a response from me.

"I'm sorry, Mother. I was so caught up in the beauty of the property, I missed your question." She paused for a moment, mildly annoyed, but repeated the question. "I asked if you have ever owned a dog before." Wow. She not only asked a question but she'd changed the subject entirely and I hadn't even noticed. "Oh, no Mother. I've never owned a dog before but have always wanted one and now I'm going to have Princeton. He's a wish come true." Princeton had been walking by my side the entire time. With each pant, vapor would emit as a smokey puff from his open mouth.

The property truly was grand in size and appearance. A very impressive piece of land, indeed. The snow was about a foot deep except in areas that had been shoveled by Ernie and Thad. Snow and icicles clung to the limbs of the trees and fence posts creating a winter wonderland affect. I was becoming tired and was ready to retreat to the warmth of the house. I sensed the same was true of Marylynn. Her conversation had dwindled to just a word here or there and I was glad of that. It had been far more tiring for me trying to pay close attention to her and to guard my every word than it had been trekking the property. Plus, I had seen enough of the property to begin devising an exit plan. A feeling of pure excitement came over me and a thrilling chill ran up my spine at the thought of freedom.

As we turned to head back toward the huge, mansion-sized house, I asked, "Mother, where does Princeton sleep at night?" She pointed toward a shed near the rear of the house. "See that garden shed? Well, there's a doggie-door where he can slip in and out at will and that's where he sleeps."

I nodded, but was glad to know where I could find him when necessary.

## CHAPTER 17

# OUTING WITH AUNT MELBA

. . . . . . . . . .

Despite the crispness of the mountain air, the day was bright and sunny. It was a perfect day for an outing. Aunt Melba's sedan was cozy on the inside from the warm air emitting from the heater. As she began her descent down the winding mountain road headed for the town below, she wasted no time initiating conversation with the boys.

"So, how the two of you been doin' lately? She asked. "I've been doin' pretty good Auntie". Thad and Ernie were both fully aware they would have to be careful about their conversation with Aunt Melba as she had unceasing interest and curiosity in discovering what Marylynn was up to and how she treated them. She had no liking for Marylynn and knew full well that the boys would hide information for fear she may confront Marylynn with anything she learned of an abusive nature. They would be protecting themselves... not Marylynn. Ernie and Thad were also aware that they oftentimes spoke before thinking which was a nagging reminder that they would need to be all the more vigilant and guarded.

But today, Aunt Melba sensed they were behaving differently

causing her to be more determined than ever to observe their every movement, their words, and patterns of behavior, hoping to discover the information they were so carefully protecting. She knew something was up.

Again, she broke the awkward silence deciding to come right out in the open with what was on her mind. "What is wrong wit the two'a you? You's never this quiet when we go on outings. I usually have to quiet you both down so I can concentrate on driving. You tell me right now what's going on." The boys remained silent. "What's wrong. The cat got your tongue?" They chuckled at that thought and in unison replied, "No". "What's that woman doin' to you boys? I've never trusted her and you boys just ain't actin' normal. What is goin' on?"

Thad spoke up, "Nothin' goin' on, Aunt Melba. We was jist talkin' so much before you got here that we's run outta stuff to say, huh Ernie?" "Yep", replied Ernie. "Oh c'mon now, you know that ain't true," snapped Aunt Melba. "Yes'm Auntie, it's true. So, how's Uncle Elmer and cousin Fran doin'?" Thad's attempt at changing the subject was successful though Melba knew what he was doing. She decided to allow him to believe it and she dropped the subject of Marylynn. She knew she'd have to move on to other subjects and wait for them to finally get back around to putting down their guards. "Well, Uncle Elmer passed away about three months back. He had some kind'a stomach ailment and it got the best of him. Poor ol' Elmer. He suffered for long enough and now he's in a betta place. No more pain to deal wit. I shore do miss him, though. And Cousin Fran...well she got married last summer and already gots a baby comin' due late spring. I don't think I ever seen her so excited."

"Where we goin' first, Aunt Melba"? "Well, how 'bout the two'a you decide that? There's the usual five and dime we always visit. There's the matinee. We could go git lunch first, if you like. There's the Skate Ranch or bowlin'. Whatch'all want'a do? It's your special day." "I say we go to the five and dime first." Thad took a knowing glance at Ernie, who was seated in the backseat. Melba noticed but said nothing. "What d'ya say, Ernie?" Ernie readily agreed and gave Thad a look of acknowledgment.

"Well then, it's settled. Off to the five and dime we go. After we're done there, it'll be just about lunch time." "Yeahhhh", the boys yelled in unison. They were beginning to loosen up and enjoy themselves, which was exactly what Thelma was hoping for. "I shore have missed you boys", Melba said with a certain tenderness that she truly felt for them. "I do wish I could see you more often." "We've missed you, too, Aunt Melba." Ernie nodded in agreement.

Finally reaching the bottom of the mountain and rounding a corner, there it was...the five and dime store. Thad and Ernie loved this store. It was always stocked with interesting, fun, cheap, items that the boys could enjoy even at home. Because things were so inexpensive, Melba was able to afford to give them a little more money to shop. Ernie and Thad immediately set to looking at the list of items Timmie had asked about. They were huddled together looking at the list so as to not allow Melba's curious eyes to see it. Melba immediately became suspicious but opted to say nothing about it but rather observe. They began whispering between the two of them. "You go that way and I'll go this way. See if you can find the compass and I'll look for the flashlight and batteries." Melba was looking at items on the shelf but had honed in on their conversation. She had heard every word.

"Here's the flashlights, Ernie. What color should we get?" "Shhh, be more quiet, Thad. She's gonna hear us. I think she'd like red," Ernie whispered. "We better get batteries too, huh?. They're over here," Thad added. Ernie nodded.

"Now, we gotta find the journals. They'll be over by the school stuff." They found the packages of lined writing paper and the journals laying right beside them. They couldn't find any that were labeled, "Journal" so they settled on a "composition" tablet. They picked one and then chose two ink pens to go with it. "Do you think she'll want two tablets, Ernie?" She only mentioned getting just one", added Ernie. "Okay".

Melba had stayed in the next aisle but directly across from them so she could hear their private conversation. She wondered who the "she" was that they had referred to. She wandered into their aisle and asked, "So what you guys have so far?" They looked a bit startled and lost for words but then Ernie spoke up. "Well, we're getting these things just for fun." "Uh huh. And what y'all gonna do wit dat flashlight"? "Sometimes when I wake up at night to use the bathroom, I can't see very good. This will help me," answered Ernie. "Plus, sometimes we go in the closet and tell scary stories. This flashlight will be good to use if we get really scared". Thad said nothing but stood there nodding his head wildly in agreement. Melba didn't ask any more questions but continued on the alert.

The boys decided it may be a bit wiser to scrap the idea of looking for a compass. They'd better stop while they're ahead and look for things that were more suited to their own interests so Melba would stop asking questions. They proceeded over to the color books and crayons. The color books they had at home were long used up and the crayons were in small broken pieces. They each picked a comic book. Thad found a kaleidoscope. He'd always been mesmerized by them. Ernie found a paint-by- number book and some water paints. They seemed happy with their selections and told Aunt Melba that they were finished shopping and were ready for lunch. Once again, Aunt Melba changed the subject to put them at ease. "You boys know that Christmas is right around the corner. It's okay to pick out more stuff to keep busy with. They continued meandering over to the check stand, stopping along the way to get a closer look at this and that. Once at the check stand, the boys each picked out a couple packs of gum and some jaw breakers. They placed their goods on the counter and as always, they made sure to thank Aunt Melba.

They enjoyed having lunch together and then went skating. Skating had piqued their appetites and they were now ready for dinner. Oh, what a wonderful day it had been. Unfortunately, it was time to go home. The drive home was very quiet. The boys knew it would be a long time before they'd see Aunt Melba again. Aunt Melba was quiet too. She knew something was amiss. But what?

## CHAPTER 18

# A WELL-TRAINED PRINCETON

· · · · · · · · · ·

Time continued marching forward and before we knew it, spring was on the horizon and the snow was slowly disappearing with the exception of an occasional flurry that didn't stick around for very long. The air was still crisp and cold, especially at night. Old Man Winter was in no hurry to give up his grip but I knew that eventually spring would have her way. Marylynn had begun to avail more and more freedoms to me. She allowed as much time out in the large courtyard as I wanted as long as I was training Princeton and as long as she was at home. All she asked was that I stay within full view of the front window. And I could walk around the house at will as long as she was home, too. Otherwise, I still spent my days and nights locked in my room. This new development was wonderful. One step forward was worth every bit of time I still spent locked in my room. And, there had been several steps made. I was biding my time and had become well accustomed to my role in the family. Marylynn seemed mostly convinced that I had no interest in anything other than pleasing her as a daughter...with only one exception, that being, training and spending time with Princeton. I

never broke any of the rules that Marylynn set for me. I was careful
to do nothing that might bring about a backwards step in my new-
found freedom. I submitted completely to her will and literally
became what she wanted me to be. It wasn't easy. I found it most
difficult to pretend as though I was not friends with the boys. They
had become very special to me and I appreciated them more than
they would ever know. They played along very well. They knew their
lives depended on it. As much as I hated to admit it, this home and
the situation had become acceptable to me in many ways. I knew
that one day I would miss certain things about it, most especially
the boys. I would be forever thankful that this beautiful "mountain
retreat", which was really nothing more than a glorified prison for
me, wasn't far worse. It sure could have been. Nonetheless, nothing
would distract me from my plans to find my way home. That indeed
would be my next venture.

I kept my countenance cheerful and to some degree, that seemed
to overflow onto Marylynn. She even treated the boys a little better
than she had in the beginning. I was putting every effort into training
Princeton and it was paying off. He was incredibly intelligent. He
understood and responded to my every command. He was such a joy
to work with. My commands to him were almost entirely by hand
signal. Seldom did I offer an audible command. I taught him this
method purposefully. He was now my dog and I would be taking
him with me one day soon.

Oh, what a lucky girl I was. Most children who are abducted are
not so lucky. Many never see home again and I didn't even want to
think of the fear, the torture, the heartache and horror so many had
gone through before ultimately being murdered. I had to thank God
for His tender mercies to me. I only wish I could have saved Bradley.

Marylynn was putting forth much effort in spending more time
at home. I wasn't sure if that was good or not but I suppose in the
long run it had its benefits. It gave me more time with Princeton and
also more time to convince Marylynn of how happy I was to be with
her. So in addition to becoming a canine trainer, in the process I'd

also become an excellent actress. So good, in fact, that I felt a great deal of guilt. I had become profoundly dishonest but really, what choice did I have?

I had been keeping a journal of all pertinent, and even what would seem to be irrelevant events, that took place on a daily basis because I wasn't sure what would be considered important once all was said and done. Maybe one day I would write a book about this experience.

Lord willing, my parents would be seeing me again soon. Oh how I wish I could say the same for sweet Bradley. At least I knew what happened to him and that he was treated well and loved deeply while in my care. I was ready for action as soon as the time was right. I had no compass but God. I would just follow the road that led down the mountain as closely as possible, taking special care to stay out of the view of passing cars. Heaven forbid Marylynn should drive by and catch me. Oh, how nice it was to finally have a plan in place. I now had a flashlight, extra batteries, warm clothes, and Princeton would be by my side. My mind raced as I thought about the reality of it all. A feeling of delight mingled with an ample amount of anxiety, I was finally seeing a light at the end of the tunnel. Oh spring, beautiful spring, come quickly.

CHAPTER 19

# FINALLY, SPRINGTIME

· · · · · · · · · ·

K nowing full well that my time here was short caused the days
to begin dragging on. Winter seemed in no hurry to leave. I
continued following the routine I had become accustomed to
and the family was no longer watching me as closely as before. They
didn't seem to be questioning my motives or intentions. Marylynn
allowed complete freedom of the home unless a visitor happened
by, which seldom occurred. The gate at the entrance to the property
was a huge deterrent; not to mention that Marylynn had no friends.
I was now allowed to stroll the property, with permission, but of
course never allowed outside the property. Marylynn said that it
was for my own safety. The one restriction she placed on me that she
never faltered on, was that I was never to watch television. *Little did
she know.* She said television was unhealthy for young minds and a
colossal waste of precious time.

Most of my spare time was spent walking and running
with Princeton. My physical endurance was at an all-time high.
Considering that I had been running through foot-deep snow
regularly made the runs grueling but it was paying off. Princeton,
too, was in maximum condition.

As we ran together, I would intermittently stop and issue a

command. Either by word or hand signal, and he would immediately obey. "Stop, sit, lay, come, heel, fetch, roll over. He knew many more commands but these would be the ones most important for him to master...and he did. Even Marylynn was impressed by his remarkable abilities. She also acknowledged my hard work and perseverance and suggested that one day I consider training seeing-eye dogs. I had to admit that was a good idea and something I could totally immerse myself into. I praised Princeton profusely and often for a job well-done and he seemed to thrive on pleasing me. He no longer required treats for a reward. He just enjoyed spending time with me and verbal praise. He waited patiently every morning for me to appear so we could begin our routine. He loved companionship and a good challenge. A dog better than Princeton simply did not exist. We were as ready as we would ever be, Princeton and me.

Then, one bright, beautiful morning, as I gazed out my bedroom window, there it was, the first robin of the spring season appeared. Snow lay only in small patches here and there and tiny leaf buds adorned the deciduous trees. A clear sign spring had arrived. The air was still very brisk but my heart was warming at the sights and very soon, the air would follow suit. Light green blades of grass were peeking from beneath the damp earth. All I needed was that perfect moment. *Patience, Timmie...patience.*

With Marylynn spending more time at home, finding that perfect opportunity may prove to be a bit more of a challenge. In an effort to discover her plans for the upcoming week, I sought Marylynn to spend some time with her. I found her in the library. The door was open only a crack and I could see her seated at the desk. I knocked lightly on the heavy wooden door. She didn't answer immediately but then she said, "Who is it"? "It's me...Loren. May I come in"? "You are welcome to enter, Loren." As I entered and glanced at Marylynn, it was fairly clear she had been weeping. Her eyes and nose were reddish and she dabbed her cheeks with a handkerchief. "How can I help you, Loren?" she said without lifting her eyes to look at me. "Oh Mother, did I come at a bad time"? Marylynn continued to gaze down at the floor. When she finally spoke, her efforts to contain her emotions were successful but she kept her face expressionless. "Mother, are you okay? Is there something I can do to help?" "No, Loren. I'll work through this moment. It's just that at times, I miss my father. Spending time in his office, sitting at his desk sometimes brings him closer to me for just a little while, in a sort of way. I'll be fine. Is there something you need?" "No, Mother, I was just hoping to spend some time with you before you have to leave again. Tomorrow being Monday, I figured you may have to leave and I'm never quite sure how long it will be before I get to see you again." "How kind of you, Loren. I actually have the next two weeks off for vacation. I will be home every day with the exception of some errands I must run and some shopping I need to get done." My heart dropped for a moment. I was so hoping she'd be leaving tomorrow. "Oh, how wonderful", I replied cheerfully. "However, I will be gone the entire week following my vacation. I will be so behind in my work by then, I'll need that week to concentrate on getting caught up. I hope you understand." "Yes, I do understand. Well then, since you will be home the next two weeks, we'll have plenty of time to spend together before you have to leave. I'll go away and leave you alone for now." "Thank you, Loren".

Wow! I had just shrewdly gleaned the information I needed. And, it was so easy. It was now the end of April so I would plan my get-away for around the second week of May. I squealed under my breath in glee...Eeeeek! It had been nearly a year since I'd seen my mom and dad and best friend, Kara. And now, the reality of reuniting with them was on the horizon. Unbelievable! "Thank you Father in Heaven. I pray your guidance and protection on me, on Princeton, and on our trek home. And thank you for paving a way for me."

Over the course of the next two weeks, Marylynn made a concerted effort to spend more time with me. My conscience was stirring a bit as I realized my utter deceit was paying off. Deceitfulness had never been a character trait I had aspired to master. But why was I feeling guilty? After all, this woman was evil. So, after much thought, I successfully convinced myself that "deceitfulness" in this instance, truly was an attribute...a form of self-preservation.

Marylynn had been coming up to my room personally each morning to invite me to join her for breakfast. My presence in this house, and the fact that Marylynn believed she finally had the daughter she'd always wanted seemed to have brought new meaning into her life. Ernie and Thad benefited to some degree from Marylynn's new found contentment, though they continued on as "help", not as family, as far as Marylynn's view of them was concerned. I missed them. It had been some time since I had spent an evening visiting with the boys and watching the news in Ernie's room.

## CHAPTER 20

# AUNT MELBA MAKES THE PHONE CALL

· · · · · · · · · ·

unt Melba sat comfortably in her easy chair watching the evening news while enjoying a bowl of chili beans with crackers and cheese. Her recent visit with the boys was still fresh in her mind. Time and again, she'd mulled over that day's events and the odd behavior of the two boys, unable to come to any solid conclusions. The only thing she was sure of is that somehow, and in some way, Marylynn was at the bottom of it all. The whole scenario made no sense. Such an odd, suspicious, curious situation, the Myers household.

She had almost accepted the fact she would never figure any of it out until, that is, the evening news came on.

Following the commercial break, Detective Bill Shore appeared. He was airing a public update on the disappearances of the Ellis girl and the Harris boy. "It is now the end of April. In two months it will be a year since Timarie Ellis disappeared and nine months since Bradley Harris was abducted. There have been no new leads of late. However, through our investigations, we are convinced that both children are very likely still alive. I am pleading with the public...

please do not allow this case to be forgotten. These unfortunate circumstances could happen to any one of our children. It doesn't just happen to someone else. Ask the Ellises, ask the Harrises. Keep vigilant in watching for any signs or sightings of either child." A picture of each child appeared on the screen. "Anything that you see, hear about, or that seems remotely suspicious, no matter how insignificant it may seem to you, may turn out to be the very lead we have been waiting for. Please call my office and ask for me directly concerning any thing you may wish to report. All reports will be followed up on. We will determine if it is a possible lead or not". His phone number appeared on the screen and Melba jotted it down... just in case, because you never know.

Melba wondered what possibly could have happened to those two unfortunate children. She walked to the kitchen to brew a cup of tea. *A twelve year old girl and a toddler boy.* Her mind was wandering. *I wonder who that journal was for. The flashlight...pens.* These were items the boys had never shown interest in before. And their behavior...truly bizarre. So secretive, whispering. *Oh Melba, don't be silly. Yer allowin' yer imagination to play tricks on ya. Just stop!*

She went back to the living room, re-positioned herself in her chair and continued watching television. But the words of Detective Shore kept coming back. "...no matter how insignificant it may seem...anything remotely suspicious." Just then, she recalled having seen the upstairs curtain move. She knew it was not the boys who had moved it since they were standing right next to her outside. And it wasn't Marylynn either, since she had just turned to go back into the house. So then, who was it?

Well that's it, she thought. What can it hurt? I may as well just call. After all, the whole thing did seem very suspicious. She picked up the phone and dialed the number. She heard one ring and quickly hung up the phone. *Naw, he'll just think I'm a silly woman for calling and bothering him about Ernie and Thad...because they was whisperin'? Because they bought a journal and a flashlight?* Then she recalled him saying that "no information will be viewed as unimportant."

Again, she picked up the phone and dialed. *Here goes nothin'*, she thought.

She froze when a male voice picked up the other end and said, "Detective Shore's office. May I help you?"

"Well, uh, I was watchin' the news just earlier about them missin' children, and you folks said to be sure and call if anyone sees anything at all suspicious." "Yes ma'am, I sure did. You're speaking with Detective Shore. Who am I speaking with?" "My name is Melba Caldwell and this may have nothin' at all to do with them missin' kids. It's probly nothin' but I guess it don't hurt to report it anyway." "Yes Ma'am. I'm glad you called. You go right ahead."

"Well, last week I went to pick up my nephew, Thad, and his best friend, Ernie for our yearly outing. Thad lives with his best friend, Ernie, and Ernie's sister, Marylynn. Oh goodness, I don't even know where to start. Anyway, both boys, well, they're actually men, but in age only. They's both mentally challenged but they's good boys. I took them down the mountain for the day. They was keepin' secrets and whisperin'. It ain't like them at all."

She proceeded to explain in detail everything that happened, right down to what they purchased and how out of character the items were that they chose.

"Miss Caldwell, what mountain are you referring to?" "They's livin' up in Big Bear with Marylynn." She continued on her rant. "What them boys want with a journal...a flashlight, batteries? Stuff like they's neva bought befoe or had any interest in. I heard'em talkin' bout a compass, but I started askin' questions so they start lookin' at stuff more suitin' to their own interests. They's hidin' something and I know it. I know them boys like the back'a my hand. There's sumpthin' goin' on and I want'a know what", she said with conviction. "They don't even know what a compass is much less how to use one. It ain't fer them, I know that fer a fact, so then who's it foe?"

She was feeling more and more comfortable sharing the information with the detective and was actually glad she'd called, even if it was insignificant information to him. It just felt good to get it all off her chest.

"Miss Caldwell, did you speak to the boy's sister about their behavior?" "Oh, dear lawd, NO! That woman is about as friendly as a shark. She ain't got no phone in the house and lawd knows it ain't because she can't afford one. She only allows me but one visit per year with my nephew and I have to write a letter in advance requesting permission and giving her a date and time. Then, I have to wait for a note of approval from her. She's very secretive and I'm never allowed to step foot inside the house. Them boys is afraid of her and fer good reason, too. She gets away wit treatin' them like her own personal slaves because they's mental. I've tried to talk my nephew into comin' and livin' wit me but he wants to stay wit his best friend. They's been best friends fer a long, long time. Bless they hearts."

"Miss Caldwell, can you tell me what kind of car this woman, this Marylynn, drives?" "Well, mostly I've seen a large black sedan of some kind parked in her garage. Maybe a Cadillac? But then one day when both garage doors was open, there was a van, of some sort...a white van parked in there." Suddenly, it occurred to her. A white van. The same description the train engineer had seen the day of the abduction.

Detective Shore didn't comment. He just asked if she could give him the address for Marylynn, which of course, she did. Aunt Melba continued, "But sir, that whole propety is fenced and gated. No vehicle can enter without the control she keeps in her car or the house opener. It's impossible to just drive up to her door unless she's expectin' you."

"I see. Well this conversation has been quite interesting, Ma'am. You will hear back from me if I think of any more questions. Oh, and Miss Caldwell, it's best to keep our conversation completely confidential at least until the information you've given me has been followed up on."

"My lips is zipped, Detective. And, I hope if you go out there to talk to Marylynn that you don't mention it was me that sent ya. It wouldn't be a good outcome for them boys."

Detective Shore gave her his word and wished her a good day.

Slightly embarrassed over the call, Aunt Melba hung up the phone. She wasn't sure if she should feel silly or if the fact that Marylynn owned a white van could prove to be a lead. She was just glad that the detective made her feel comfortable and listened to what she had to say with interest.

Det. Shore had taken plenty of notes and he had a gut feeling about the information Melba had shared. It was the same feeling he was accustomed to getting when he'd gotten a new lead and knew he was on the right track. He hung up the phone and shouted into the adjoining office, "I might have just gotten the break I've been waiting for on the Ellis, Harris, cases." "No way", was the reply. "Yep. Gotta do a little footwork first but very soon I'll be taking a drive up the mountain headed to Big Bear. Who wants to join me?" Again, the same voice replied, "I'll go...as long as we can grab some donuts and coffee before heading up".

## CHAPTER 21

# AFTER THE FINAL VISIT ...

· · · · · · · · · ·

Finally, the evening before Marylynn was to return to work had come. It had turned out to be a pleasant two weeks. We had gotten along quite well...Marylynn and me. I'd given her no reason to ever doubt me as I'd been a model daughter for her. She'd be leaving very early in the morning before I ever woke up. Tonight may very well be the last time I see Marylynn under the current conditions. So, I made sure to wish her a safe trip and tell her I'd miss her. To this day, she'd mentioned nothing at all to me about where she worked or what she did for a living. Knowing Marylynn as I did, I just knew I shouldn't ask. She had no idea that I was already fully aware of her occupation. I wished her "good night" as I intended to go to bed early. I needed time to think and to fine-hone my plans and convince myself I was really ready. The very thought of leaving the house in the middle of the night and disappearing into the utter darkness of the cold, immense forest, with wild and dangerous animals lurking about, caused immense fear to well up inside me. I began to feel anxious and afraid and wondered for just a moment if I'd actually be able to follow through. But I knew I would. I had to.

I had waited too long for this day and had been planning for it for what felt like an eternity. I would definitely be going. But along with the fear came a feeling of exhilaration. My thoughts and emotions were all over the place. Would I even be able to sleep tonight? I reminded myself that Princeton would be with me and that thought offered a bit of solace. I took a slow, deep, breath in an effort to relax and calm myself. I let the air out slowly and repeated the process.

Once I was confident that Marylynn was in her own room for the night, I slipped down the hallway to Ernie's door, tapped lightly and said good night. I did the same as I passed Thad's door. As always, they both quickly responded with, "Good night, Loren." I was going to miss these two so I wanted to make the very best of the time we had left together.

Next morning, I was awakened by a tap at my door. "Miss Loren, are you awake, can we come in?" The boys had missed me during the weeks Marylynn was home. We'd had very little contact but now Marylynn was gone. "Well of course. Come on in." The door burst open and they came in wearing big smiles. "Good morning, Miss Loren. We missed you so much." "I missed you too. How are you guys doing?" "We're doing better now that Marylynn is gone", answered Ernie with a chuckle. "We don't have breakfast ready yet but we just wanted to see you first thing", continued Ernie.

"Hey, I'm glad you did. How about we all go down and make breakfast together and then eat in the dining room? Don't worry, Marylynn will never know." I laughed which made them laugh, too.

I was thinking to myself how this morning may be the last time we have breakfast together. I wanted it to be special. I actually had to fight back tears at the thought. They'd been so good to me...so kind, and they trusted me.

"Okay, so what should we make? Don't know about you guys but I'm in the mood for strawberry blintz. What do you guys say?" "Ooh, that sounds mighty good to me, Miss Loren" responded Thad. Ernie added, "Yeah...sounds mighty good." "Now, all we gotta do is make sure we have everything we need to make it." "Oh, we do, Miss Loren", Ernie said assuredly.

We busied ourselves in the kitchen and as we sat down at the beautiful dining room table to enjoy breakfast, I suggested we say a prayer first and thank God for the blessings He gives us. Ernie and Thad looked at each other. I wondered if they were uncomfortable with saying a prayer but then Thad said, "Miss Loren, I like that idea. I remember when me and Ernie was going to that special school, every day before lunch our teacher would say a prayer to thank God for our food. Marylynn never prays and me and Ernie haven't prayed for a long time." "Well, that settles it. We'll pray today." I wanted desperately to pray for the protection and well-being of these two boys as I had no idea what would become of them once I was gone and Marylynn, apprehended. I didn't want to pray in such a way as to cause them alarm or to alert them to anything at all. I bowed my head and folded my hands and with eyes closed I began to pray. "Oh Dear Heavenly Father. We come to you this morning in thankfulness that we can enjoy each other's company and this delicious breakfast together. I want to ask that you will always and forever guide and protect Ernie and Thad. Father, they are such good, decent men, and have been such good friends to me. They're always so kind to me and I appreciate them and I thank you for bringing them into my life. And thank you for this food and for this beautiful day. Help us to spend the day well in doing things that will be pleasing in your sight. Please help Marylynn to be kind to them and to never cause them harm or to be afraid. We ask your blessings on all of us and that you will help us to be worthy of those blessings. In Jesus' name, Amen".

As I finished praying and looked up at the boys, I noticed tears had welled up in their eyes. They were appreciative of the kind words of affection with regard to them. They were starved for acknowledgment, kindness and appreciation for all they'd offered in the way of help around the house and property. Marylynn never gave them credit for a job well done but was quick to punish and condemn them for anything she could find that may not be up to her own personal standard.

They seemed a bit embarrassed about the tears so I pretended not to notice. "Okay, let's get to eating." All that could be heard after that was forks hitting the plates. Oh, the blintzes were so good. These two boys were excellent cooks. I was going to miss this, as well. Breakfast was delightful. I helped with clean-up. And now we had the whole day ahead of us.

"So, would you guys like to see all the tricks I've taught Princeton?" "Sure would", they agreed. We all proceeded outside. I called Princeton and he came loping over to us, tail wagging, greeting each of us. I proceeded to call out each command and like always, Princeton responded well. I instructed the boys in how to use hand signals to get him to respond. They were amazed and enjoyed seeing all the progress Princeton had made. Being allowed to take part added a special feature to it all. We then took a walk around the property and conversed as we went. I made sure to take special notice of the hole under the fence. I hoped I could fit under it without too much trouble.

At lunch time, we prepared a picnic lunch and ate out in the courtyard. The weather was cool but not uncomfortably so. After that, we watched a movie together, which made us tired so we decided to take a nap...in the living room. Marylynn would have been livid. I took the white love seat and the boys took opposite ends of the white sofa. Of course, we removed our shoes so there would be no tell-tale signs left behind. We thought of every way we could to step outside the lines and break all the rules we could without leaving any tracks behind. It was fun. The boys laughed and giggled all day.

That night, we all watched the news together. There she was, Marylynn, reporting on several items of public interest. Included toward the end of the broadcast was a clip of Detective Shore sharing with the television audience an update on the Harris/Ellis cases. He stated that there was no sign, to date, of the missing children but that new leads were still trickling in.

The camera focused back onto Marylynn, who was smiling smugly, confident that nothing the public had to offer would be of any value. She was convinced that she had covered her tracks quite adequately.

I was curious to know what kind of leads had been offered. I had to agree with Marylynn, though. What could the public possibly have to offer at this late stage of the game? The case had pretty much gone cold but I was thankful that we had not been forgotten. The detective on the case was refusing to give up. But, if all went according to plan, I would be thanking him very soon for his efforts.

The boys and I had enjoyed a wonderful, fun-filled day of freedom. We'd taken full advantage of Marylynn's absence for the first time ever. Dinner came and went. Despite the fact that we'd all had a nap earlier in the day, the boys were worn out from all the unusual activities. Night had come and it was nearing 10:00. This was about the time they usually would begin to ready themselves for bed. They had determined to stay up later than usual because they didn't want the day to end. But I was ready for the day to end. I had somewhere I had to go. So, I suggested we watch a movie after the news, knowing they wouldn't be as interested in it as I was. Their eyes began to get heavy. Try as they might, they could hardly keep their eyes open. Soon, they fell deeply asleep. Gently, I slipped off the bed and stood there, just looking down at them as they slept. My heart cried a little knowing what my intentions had been in tricking them to fall asleep earlier than they had wanted to. I began gathering what was left of the snacks we had brought up to eat while watching television. There was cheese and crackers, one muffin left, and some orange juice. I took the items to my room where I proceeded to remove my pillow case from my pillow and stuff the items into it. There was some bottled water on my end table so I threw that in as well. I reached deeply between the mattresses of the bed and retrieved the diary that was hidden there, placing it under my shirt and then tucked my shirt into my pants. I wouldn't dare forget my own journal, pens, flashlight and batteries. I hesitated for a moment, thinking I heard movement coming from the boys room. All was quiet so I continued. I slipped into the gear I had readied earlier. I pulled my sweater over my head, put sweat pants on over my jeans, put on my warmest jacket and my pink knit cap and gloves. I was already wearing my snow boots with extra socks, but I threw a couple pairs of socks into the pillow cover in case of an emergency.

A million thoughts raced through my head. The boys would be overcome with grief when they found me gone in the morning. They would be fearful of what Marylynn would do to them when she discovered they had allowed me to escape. They will think I betrayed them. But I knew I would be sending help for them and that Marylynn would never have the opportunity to harm them. I decided to take a moment to write a simple note to them.

"Dear Ernie and Thad. I had to go but will see you soon. Do not be afraid. I am sending help for you. I love you both very much. Thank you for everything. Please don't be upset with me.

Love, Timmie."

I slung the pillowcase full of items over my shoulder, turned off the light, and quietly tip-toed down the hallway to Ernie's room. The boys were snoring quietly so I knew they would not hear me. I left the note on Ernie's chest of drawers, placing a half-filled glass of water on the corner of it so it couldn't drop to the floor and disappear under something.

I had to go back to steal one last look at the room I had been kept secluded in for nearly a year. My time here with Marylynn and the boys had truly been bittersweet. I knew I would somehow miss certain things that I had become accustomed to over the course of time, but certainly not enough to keep me here...not even close. My mind wandered back to Carrie. *Don't worry, Carrie. Your death will be vindicated soon. I am so sorry for what you had to go through at the hands of Marylynn. I am sorry for the way your life ended. I wish there had been some way I could have helped you. I have your diary with me. You will have a voice and Marylynn will pay.*

I turned to leave and then thought of Bradley. I felt tears welling up in my eyes. I would be breaking the news of his death to his parents very soon. I must keep moving forward. I entered the darkened hallway and tip-toed passed Ernie's bedroom. Took one last glance at the sleeping boys and continued down the stairs headed toward the front door of the house. *I can't believe I'm actually doing this.*

I carefully pulled open the door. The outside air was crisp and cold and the night was very dark as the tall pines prevented even the slightest amount of moonlight to reach the ground. I pulled the flashlight out of the bag and headed in the direction of Princeton's shed. I softly spoke his name, as I didn't want him to be startled thinking there was an intruder and come out barking. I whistled softly...phhht, phhht, "Princeton...c'mon boy. Let's go". Out he came, his head cocked to one side as this was a highly unusual situation. His tail was wagging as he was ready for play time no matter the time of day...or night. "C'mon Boy", I prompted as I headed toward the chain link fence.

Finally, here it was. I pulled back the brush from around the dug out area and motioned for Princeton to go through. He was happy to oblige and once on the other side, he waited patiently for me to follow. I got down on my hands and knees and tried to fit through but it was proving a bit more challenging than expected. I found a rock and began to use it to dig the hole a bit deeper and wider. Princeton began digging on the other side of the fence. His intelligence and extraordinary common sense never failed to amaze me.

Again I tried to crawl under, this time catching my jacket on the pointed edge at the bottom of the fence. I didn't let that stop me. I pushed with my toes and pulled my way through, grabbing shrubbery, roots, rocks...anything I could get a firm grip on to pull myself completely through. I tore my jacket doing it, but I got through to the other side. Hallelujah!

Now, as I stood to my feet, I was literally in the forest. I was off Marylynn's property and vulnerable to whatever awaited me in the darkness of these immense woods. I was overwhelmed for a moment but the thought that Marylynn could actually come home and catch me drove me onward. "C'mon Princeton, let's go." I began walking in the direction I knew led down hill. My eyes had grown a bit accustomed to the darkness so I decided to use my flashlight as little as possible. I had no idea how long it would take me to get down this mountain and I would not want to run out of batteries and have no light when needed.

The forest was dark and scary, but I knew ahead of time it was going to be. I would do my best not to dwell on that. Princeton remained right by my side leaning in to me with his warm body every step, as I knew he would. He didn't seem concerned at all, so why should I be? Sticks and branches cracked and rustled beneath our feet. An owl hooted...such an eerie sound in the darkness of the forest. This was going to be a long night. I was glad I'd taken a nap earlier in the day. I caught my toe on something and stumbled to the ground. The forest floor was damp and cold and covered with pine needles. I could hear an occasional vehicle drive by going one direction or the other. How I wished I could ask someone for a lift down the hill, but I dared not take such a chance. Any one of those cars could be Marylynn, or Heaven forbid...someone even more evil than she. Staying hidden under the cover of darkness and taking my chances with wild animals was a better bet.

We increased our pace in an effort to make better time. The intense workouts that Princeton and I had been doing was surely paying off. We walked on, down valleys and across shallow brooks. My boots were rubber and reached almost to my knees which protected my feet and legs from the frigid mountain waters. Princeton took a long drink.

I snagged my cap on a low branch and it was abruptly pulled from my head. It happened so quickly that I was gripped with fear for a moment thinking that someone had grabbed my cap off of me. My heart pounded rapidly as adrenaline flowed through my body like a jet stream. I could barely breathe. My fear of Marylynn was so great that I could almost see her at every turn. Realistically however, it would be highly unlikely she would ever come into the forest at night to try and find me. She might send the boys but even that was unlikely...and I had no fear of them. I remembered wondering if this night would ever arrive but now I was wondering if it would ever end. I turned, grabbed my cap from the dry, skinny little branch that had stolen it from me and pulled it back on to my head and over my ears, and continued on. I was becoming discouraged, as some of the valleys were so low and the trek back up the other side so steep- was it even realistic that we'd ever make it down the mountain?

Eventually we stopped to rest. There was no sign of morning light. I had no idea what time it was or how long we'd been walking. I found a log to sit on. My legs were feeling the stress of all the walking and climbing. But as we sat there catching our breaths, the sounds of the forest became more audible. We were sitting motionless so when I heard branches snapping, I knew it was not me or Princeton. There it was again, snapping...rustling. Princeton's ears perked up. Now, I was concerned. Princeton lowered his head, and turned toward the direction of the noise, just listening. There it was again, rustling in the brush off to our right. Princeton emitted a low, quiet growl. He suddenly sprang to his feet as though preparing for attack. He barked loud and suddenly, which startled me but must also have startled whatever was lurking out there because something took off running to beat the wind. The sound of running continued until it finally became so faint we could no longer hear it. I figured it must have been a deer. Princeton settled down and once again, we were on our way.

A gentle breeze had begun to whistle through the trees causing the air to feel colder. I knew we were still headed in the proper direction as I could actually see the vehicle headlights from time to time. The road was now several yards above the area we were walking.

Several times I noticed sets of glowing eyes peering at us from the dark recesses of the forest. They were likely nothing more than the curious eyes of raccoon, deer, opossums and the like. We heard coyotes howling off in the distance. The sights and sounds of the forest had become a bit less frightening now than when we had first set off on our journey. We walked for what seemed like hours and still no sign of a morning sun. I was finally exhausted and knew I would have to stop shortly and take a long-overdue, rest. I didn't want to fall asleep while it was still night time.

At last, I saw the glow of what would soon be the sun peaking over the horizon. Princeton and I had traveled all night long. I spotted a large fallen log further down the hill a ways, nestled in what appeared to be a dry gully. It looked like a good place to take a rest. We made our way toward it and once there I took a seat, then positioned myself horizontally. Oh, it felt good to lie down and put my feet up. I looked up at the early morning sky. It was barely showing signs of daylight. I wanted to fall asleep but was afraid someone might happen along and see me. Princeton collapsed in a heap at the foot of the log and promptly fell asleep. I was glad for him and decided to allow him a much needed and deserved nap. I knew that if Princeton felt comfortable enough to fall asleep, that all was well and safe for me to also relax for awhile.

The sky was beautiful and blue. The air was beginning to warm just a bit. I wondered how much longer it would take us to reach the bottom of the mountain. It might take us days. Then I began to think. *Oh no. What will I do once we reach the bottom. Where will I go. Who will I ask for help.* These were issues I had not thoroughly thought out. *Oh well, I guess I'll just have to work it out once I get there.*

I must have dropped off to sleep at some point despite my determination not to, because I found myself waking up some time later. I believed it was still morning because the sun was still fairly low. I had a feeling I was being watched and when I turned to look, there sat Princeton watching me. He'd been waiting quietly and patiently for me to wake up. "Thank God it's you, Princeton. Good morning, Boy." He let out a little whine and began to pant a little. I knew he must be hungry and so was I. I opened the bag and took out the crackers. We shared some of them along with some cheese. After taking a few sips of water, we once again started out on our journey. I thought of Ernie and Thad. Surely they knew by now that I was gone. I wondered if they'd noticed that Princeton was gone as well.

The sunshine effectively diminished the eeriness of the dark forest and had replaced it with singing, chirping birds, chattering squirrels, and other creatures and sounds natural to the forest in the day-time. It was a beautiful day. The sound of the traffic had increased along with the warmth of the morning sun. It was a perfect day for a homecoming. I smiled at the thought. Up ahead, I noticed a large clearing where the forest trees were sparse and few. Only large boulders would be available to use as cover, unless I went further down into the valley where the forest became thick again. That would take a lot of extra walking and would present a very real chance of becoming lost. I decided not to do that. "Well Princeton, it's going to be tricky but I think we can do it. We'll just race from one boulder to the next between intermittent vehicles until we reach the thicker forest again. Are we up for it? Once we reach that area, when I say run, we'll make a run for it."

## CHAPTER 22

# THE AWAKENING

· · · · · · · · · ·

As the morning sunlight began to fill Ernie's bedroom, he began to stir around, stretching his feet out toward the end of his bed. His feet bumped into something and he halfway sat up to see what the obstruction was. "Hey, what'cha doin' on my bed, Thad? How come yer not in yer own bed?" Thad tried to open his eyes but the sunlight was hitting his face directly. He covered his face with the blanket. "I dunno. I must'a fell asleep in here. I din't mean to," he answered.

The television was still on. "Oh yeh, I remember now. We was all watchin' the news with Miss Loren." "Yeh, that's what we was doin'." answered Thad. "Guess we better be getting' up and get breakfast going. Marylynn is still gone so it's gonna be another fun day." said Ernie. They smiled and raced to Loren's room to see who could get there first...just like they used to do when she'd first arrived at their home. When they reached Loren's room, they noticed the door was open and sunlight filtered through her room and into the dim hallway. She was not on her bed. "Maybe she's in the bathroom." They tapped at her door but there was no answer forthcoming from Loren. Their eyes grew large as they looked at each other and the smiles left their faces. Her bed was fully made and looked as though it had not been slept in. They were quiet for a moment and then Ernie said, "Maybe she's in the kitchen. Maybe she wanted to surprise us with breakfast." "Let's go see" answered Thad. They turned toward the staircase and headed to the kitchen. As they approached the kitchen door and gently swung it open, they found the kitchen empty and quiet. No sign of Loren. Fear and loneliness overcame them. Their eyes filled with tears. Ernie sobbed and Thad began to cry out loud. "What we gonna do, Ernie? Marylynn gonna kill us when she gets home. Why did Loren run away? I thought she liked it here. She said she loved me and you." They walked to the front door, opened it and called out Loren's name. Then they called Princeton's name. No response. They called again. Still, no response from either Loren or Princeton. He was gone, too. "What we gonna do, Ernie?" Thad repeated. Ernie didn't answer. He just shut the front door and started up toward his room. Thad followed. "I have to think about this. Maybe we gonna have to run away too, Thad. But, what will we eat and where will we live? I don't know what to do. Let's just stay in my room for now, okay?" "Okay, ." They slowly climbed the stairs, not speaking a word. As they walked into the room, Ernie noticed the note on his chest of drawers. "Look Thad. A note. It's from Loren...I mean, Timmie." "Read it, Ernie." Ernie read the note aloud. When he finished reading he said, "I wonder what she means that she will see us soon and that she will send help?" He laid the note back where he'd found it. They only had each other now. They huddled together on the floor next to the bed. They were in the comfort of Ernie's room. They never made breakfast. They'd lost their appetites. Now, they just wondered what the days ahead held in store for them. How would they ever live without Miss Loren? She alone is what kept them going every day.

## CHAPTER 23

# HOMEBOUND

· · · · · · · · · ·

Detective Shore had arrived to work bright and early and was ready and anxious for the drive up Big Bear Mountain. He still had that gut feeling about this particular lead and it had grown even stronger over the last couple days. He'd found it hard to sleep the night before.

"Hey Chuck!" he called out. "Let's get going. If you still insist on stopping for the donuts and coffee you mentioned yesterday, you'd better get out here or I'm leaving without ya." "Hold on to your drawers, Bill. I'm comin'. What's the big hurry anyway? It's only been a year since you took this case." In reality, Chuck knew that Bill was deeply involved and concerned with breaking this case and rescuing the children. And, he wanted to be there to see it all go down. He wasted no time in joining Bill. They climbed inside one of the unmarked white detective vehicles that had all the bells and whistles on it. Big side mirrors. Several antennas strategically placed here and there. Though it was unmarked, it was an obvious law enforcement vehicle. First stop was the donut shop. Bill figured, Oh well, as long as we're here I may as well get a couple donuts and coffee too. Soon, they were on the road. Chuck took out a map, looking for the quickest route up the mountain. He said, "You know, the back route might be the quickest." That sounded good to Bill so they took to the highway and continued until they reached the base of the mountains. They'd been talking and joking until they began to ascend the mountain. Bill became quiet. His thoughts were on the children. He so hoped he would find them alive and well by some miracle of God. He began to share with Chuck some of the things that Melba had said to him about Marylynn. From the way Melba described her, she sounded like a classic example of someone capable of committing a crime of this type. His hopes were high that he was finally on the trail of the abductor(s).

The road had narrowed in some areas and had become more winding. The forest was now becoming thicker and thicker as the trees and brush growth had extended nearer to the road than before. Rocks and gullies were appearing and it was obvious that they were nearing Big Bear Lake itself. The smell of the pines filled the interior of the vehicle through the open windows. The smell was pleasant and the air, clean and crisp. Much clearer than the smoggy air at the bottom of the mountain.

Suddenly, Bill hit his brake as he noticed something move and then quickly disappear behind a boulder. He craned his neck to look back. "Hey Chuck, did you see that?" "See what?" "Never mind". He continued up the road a little further until he found a spot to turn around and head back down the mountain. "What'd you see, Bill?" "I don't know but I swear it looked like a kid and a dog." "What would a kid and a dog be doing out here alone?" retorted Chuck. "That's my question. I'm going to check it out. Just a few yards ahead is where I think I saw something off to the right." Both detectives began to scour the landscape for any sign of anybody around. "Okay, see that boulder? That's where I saw it." He pulled the car over to the side of the road and parked. "If there's anyone behind there, eventually they'll have to come out." They continued to sit there quietly, engine running. "I don't see anything", Chuck said quietly. "Just a minute, Chuck...there, look. See that?" Princeton's tail appeared from behind the rock and then part of his body. It quickly disappeared again. "Aw, It's just a dog, Bill. C'mon, let's go". "Naw, I don't think so. I think there's someone else hiding behind that boulder along with that dog." He opened the car door and exited, heading in the direction of the boulder...and the dog.

"Oh no, Princeton. We've been spotted by someone."

Detective Shore whistled to Princeton. "C'mere Boy. C'mon. I won't hurt you." Princeton wagged his tail and started to obey but then I quietly commanded him to "Sit, stay". He immediately turned back to me and obeyed the command.

No amount of coaxing proved effective. Princeton refused to obey the detective. Both officers began to cautiously approach the boulder. "Keep your eye on that rock, Chuck. I'm certain there is someone hidden behind it and it may not be a kid." Both officers placed their hands on their side piece for caution's sake and continued their approach. The closer they came to the boulder, the easier it was to see over it and finally, there appeared the top of a pink knit cap.

Shore shouted toward the rock, "Whoever is hiding behind that boulder, slowly step out into the open. We're police officers. Step out right now!" Hands on their weapons, they continued to approach. Slowly, the knit cap began to move over to the edge of the boulder until, to their surprise, out stepped a young girl looking frightened and helpless. The dog remained by her side.

Detective Shore immediately recognized her. "Would you look at this...are you Timarie Ellis?" Tears began to pour down my face as I nodded, yes, and realized who he was. I immediately recognized him from watching the news.

There she stood, the little girl he'd been looking for, for almost a year. He couldn't believe his eyes. He hurried over to where she stood, wrapped his arms around her and wept. "Hey Chuck, if I'm dreaming, don't tell me. I don't want to wake up. God in Heaven... thank you. You have no idea how happy I am to see you, young lady. It's so wonderful to know that you are alive and well. This might just be the very best day of my whole life," he said to her, grinning from ear to ear.

"I thought I might never see my parents again. I have so much to tell you. I don't know where to start. Little Bradley Harris didn't make it" I said, sobbing.

"Aw, c'mon sweetie. Let's get you home. But first stop…the Police station. You can tell me all about it on the way. Officer Chuck, here"…as he motioned to the other officer, "will call and have your parents made aware that you are alive and well and that we are bringing you in. They will be waiting for us at the office by the time we arrive."

Detective Shore suggested that Chuck drive. Princeton was coaxed into the front seat where he perched himself proudly. Detective Shore sat in back with me so I could share more details with him.

I proceeded to pour out a wealth of information as though I may never get another chance. I told him all about Marylynn Myers and her brother, Ernie, and his friend, Thad. I explained the relationship between the boys and Marylynn and how none of this was their fault, and how they'd always treated me with such kindness.

## CHAPTER 24

# FAMILY REUNION

· · · · · · · · · ·

etective Shore did not communicate the news of Timarie with headquarters by way of dispatch. He was aware that the general public may intercept the information that way. He wanted everything to be kept utterly concealed from the public. It was important even for my parents to keep this new development a secret until the time was right to share it publicly. He had a plan. He spoke with the Chief directly and explained he would share the plan with him as soon as he made it in.

As we approached the city, I began to recognize the familiar sights that I hadn't seen for so long. Princeton kept a close eye on me from his position in the front seat. He kept turning around to make sure I was still there. He was thirsty and panting with his tongue hanging out. Chuck looked over at him and assured him, "We'll be getting you some water and food in just a couple minutes, Buddy." He reached over and scratched Princeton's chest.

There it was, a building with a big sign on the front..."Police Headquarters". My heart began pounding with excitement as I knew I'd be seeing Mom and Dad in just a few short moments. The excitement was overwhelming. I started sobbing tears of joy at the very thought.

Chuck drove around to a back entrance and into a large garage. The door slid open. For a moment, I thought of Marylynn's garage door and how I'd heard it slide open when I first arrived there.

We entered the garage and the door slid shut behind us, just like the experience with Marylynn. I shuddered for a moment. As we exited the car, a voice came over the speaker in the garage. "Welcome home, Timarie Ellis." I smiled, trying to hold back more tears that I knew were inevitable.

Officer Shore opened a heavy door and we all entered a hallway with doors on either side. Princeton and I followed behind. He opened another door and motioned for me to enter. To my utter amazement, there sat Mom and Dad. "OHHH! MAMA...DADDY!" We ran to each other's open arms and we hugged and cried like we might never stop. I wailed as I held on to them tightly. Then, I started to laugh. "I'm so happy. I love you both and I have missed you so much. I thought I might never see you again." I called Princeton over and introduced him to my parents. "Princeton has been my best friend. He stayed by my side when I needed him. I have so much to tell you that I don't even know where to start. How is Trish?" "Oh Honey, you're back home now safe and sound. We'll have all the time in the world now to hear all about what happened," Mom assured.

The office door opened and a small group of officers appeared. They began to applaud and chuckle with joy at the sight of me and Princeton. They offered kind words of gladness that we were home and safe. Someone standing behind them pushed their way through with several large pizzas in hand. They smelled heavenly and it had been nearly a year since I'd had pizza. They also brought water and dog food for Princeton but he wanted pizza instead. So Pizza is what he got.

Someone from behind me said my name. I turned to see Trish standing in the doorway. "TRISH..." I ran to her and hugged her so hard she grunted. We both started laughing. "Oh Trish, how I have missed you." "I've missed you too...and thought about you every single day. I'm so glad you're back and you're okay". Tears welled up in her eyes and mine. Detective Shore said, "We decided to invite Trish and her parents to come to this long-awaited reunion because we knew how much it would mean to you, Timarie. They know the importance of keeping it all confidential until the right time, which we will be announcing when the time is right." "Thank you so much. It does mean a lot to me." Then I looked back at Trish. "Well, look at you. You must have grown two inches taller since I saw you last." "It's all that sleeping I was doing before you left", she answered with a smile.

Oh, what a dream come true. I could hardly believe I was home.

## CHAPTER 25

# ARREST OF THE ANCHORWOMAN

· · · · · · · · · ·

Detective Shore had gathered a wealth of information from me and was now armed with all the data necessary to follow through with the plans he had laid to apprehend Marylynn Myers. He knew that she would be reporting the evening news. He'd devised a plan to submit a "surprise" news update for her to report. The news would be aired in an hour. All necessary law enforcement personnel were in position up in Los Angeles and were waiting for the signal to converge on the reporting studio. He had a bit of a vendetta against her and this would be his form of revenge. She had succeeded in evading detection for nearly a year. She had been the reason for many hours of sleep deprivation along with torment at his failure to uncover new leads. She had caused his excellent reputation to be called into question. This he took personally. For someone as prideful as Marylynn Myers, the humiliation of being arrested in front of the whole world would be far worse than a death sentence. Well, she was about to pay for her sins.

Everyone who had attended our little reunion was asked to remain at the office until the news could be aired. At long last, it was that time. A television had been brought into the office and set up so everyone could easily view the screen. Trish and her family, as well as my parents, had no idea why we were asked to stay and watch the news. They just thought that it was going to be a general announcement and the police wanted them there to share in the joy of hearing it announced to the public for the first time.

The news anchorman came on and stated, "The evening news will begin shortly following this brief commercial break".

Then, there she was- Marylynn. "Marylynn Myers here with a special report and update on the disappearance of the Ellis girl." Her brow furrowed ever so slightly and a bit of concern showed in her face as she began to read the report. She glanced up at the camera and back down at the report that had just been handed to her. "This just in", she began hesitantly. "The case of the missing girl, Timarie Ellis, has been solved. She was rescued today thanks to a recent lead"...her voice tapered off and she abruptly quit speaking. Her face turned completely pale and her hands began to quiver. Her usual smug expression had vanished from her face and was promptly replaced by a look of abject fear. Her eyes grew wider and her jaw dropped slightly. She sat unsteadily on her stool and appeared faint. She quickly looked around at the back of the room to see if anyone in uniform was present. Indeed they were. Two officers approached her from behind, each taking hold of one of her arms. Her hands were placed behind her back and handcuffs were secured to her wrists by one officer while the other read her her rights. They lead her out of the news room, leaving the room empty and completely silent with no one seated at the podium. The television screen went black temporarily and then came back on. The anchorman, who was now seated where Marylynn had been, had no idea what was going on. He tried his best to keep the program moving with as little attention brought to what had just happened as possible. He hastily announced they were going to a commercial break.

The group of officers in the room broke out in applause. My parents had, more or less, figured out what it was all about but Trish's parents looked bewildered. They didn't understand what they had just witnessed on the news. I leaned over to them and said, "it was Marylynn Myers, the news anchorwoman, who abducted me and was holding me captive all this time. Don't worry...I'll tell you the whole story once we're all home." They stood there in utter disbelief at what I'd just told them. All Peggy could say was, "Seriously?" I nodded.

Marylynn had finally been caught. Never again would she be able to hurt or abuse anyone else. Somehow, as I witnessed the televised arrest of Marylynn, an odd feeling of sadness came over me. How could a woman be so sick, so insane, as to do the things she did believing she would never be caught? I was so glad to be home again and yet so sad for Ernie and Thad. I had grown very fond of both of them. They felt like family, in a sort of way to me, almost like little brothers and I was used to seeing them every day. I was going to miss them very much.

Then it hit me. The boys must have witnessed her arrest, as well. They're probably frantic wondering what is going to become of them. I turned to Detective Shore and asked him what was to become of the boys and when would someone be going out to help them.

"Don't worry, Timarie. I have that covered. There's someone out there picking them up as I speak."

I felt a huge sense of relief. "Thank you".

## CHAPTER 26

# RESCUING THE BOYS

· · · · · · · · · ·

Meanwhile, as I enjoyed a pizza party and reunion with my family and friends, a black-and-white police unit was on the way up Big Bear Mountain in route to the home of Ms. Marylynn Myers. The light bar flickered with red and blue lights but the siren was silent...at the request of Aunt Melba. She had been made aware of the entire situation and had agreed to meet the officers at the house. She knew the boys would be frightened with all the new developments and the last thing they needed to hear was the blare of sirens. The police had no intentions of making any arrests. They were fully aware of the mental status of both men and that they were innocent of willful wrongdoing. Aunt Melba would be taking both of them under her wing and accepting custody. She knew this was going to mean making some serious adjustments to her own way of life but she loved them and was more than willing to do whatever needed to be done.

Finally, the unit made the left turn into the driveway that led to the home. Aunt Melba had arrived and was waiting at the gate. Ernie and Thad were huddled in the house. Alerted by the sound of tires on gravel they began to panic, thinking that it was the police coming to take them to jail. Hidden behind the curtains, they peered out of the upstairs bedroom window. They had seen Marylynn's arrest on television so they knew it could not be her at the gate. Knowing this gave them a sense of relief, because they didn't want to end up at the bottom of the lake. Neither did they want to go to jail.

The police, using a megaphone, began to speak to the them. "This is the police, Ernie...Thad. We need you to open the gate. We are not here to hurt you. Please open the gate so we can help you". Ernie whispered to Thad, "it's a trick. They want us to open the gate so they can come get us and take us to jail". Thad replied, "Well Ernie, maybe it's not a trick. Remember Loren said she would send help...remember?" Ernie thought about it and replied, "well, let's just wait and see what else they say". They both stayed quiet and refused to respond.

Aunt Melba approached the officer, "Here, let me try. They aren't afraid of me." The officer handed the megaphone to her.

"Ernie and Thad, it's Aunt Melba here. You needs to open the gate. It's okay. You knows you can trust Aunt Melba. No one out here's gonna hurt ya. I give you my promise. You gone come home wit me." She waited a moment and when there was no response she continued. "C'mon boys, you wastin' time." This time with more insistence and a slight bit of irritation in her voice. "Let's go to the five and dime and then out to lunch, okay? C'mon, let's go... right now. If I gots to say it again, we ain't goin' nowhere."

The gate made a sudden loud screeching noise as it began to open. Aunt Melba smiled at the officer. "I knew that would work. They love that five and dime."

The vehicles slowly began moving over the gravel entry toward the property until they reached the cobblestone driveway. The front door of the house slowly opened and there stood Ernie and Thad. They looked frightened, with faces still wet with tears. They stepped out onto the porch waiting for the next order.

The officers approached Ernie and Thad. As the officers drew near, Ernie spoke to them. "We're sorry for what we done. We never wanted to hurt no one," he began to sob.

In a kind, gentle voice, one of the officers replied, "We know that none of this is your fault. Timarie Ellis told us all about what happened and that you never wanted to be involved. She told us how kind you've both been to her and also to Bradley. In fact, she gave me a note that she asked me to give to both of you.

"Will you read it for us?" asked Thad. "Sure I will. It says, 'Dear Ernie and Thad, I miss both of you so much. I want to thank you for all the wonderful and delicious meals you made for me while I was with you. I don't know what I would have done without you guys. And thank you for always being so kind to me. You're both the greatest and I consider you to be some of the best friends a girl could ever have.

Some time real soon, I am going to come visit you at your Aunt Melba's house. You can meet my parents and see Princeton again. I will never, ever, forget you.

Love, Timmie

P.S. Now you can call me by my real name. :)'

The officer smiled at them as he handed the letter to Ernie. Ernie gently reached for the letter, and with a grin, folded it and tucked it into his pocket.

In an effort to break the somberness of the moment, Aunt Melba blurted, "Alright now, enough of all the snivelin'. C'mon, I'm hungry. Let's get outta here." She coaxed Ernie and Thad into the car, wished the officers a good day, and started the engine. Ernie and Thad, now smiling, rolled down their windows so they could wave wildly, and shout "goodbye" to the officers. As Melba drove out onto the gravel driveway, she mentioned that the officers would be paying them all a visit soon to ask them a lot of questions about what happened. "Dey gonna want'a know everything dat evil woman been up to. I know'd all along she was up to no good. Lawd, dat woman's evil. I'm not sure I even want to know 'bout all the stuff she been doin'," she added.

## CHAPTER 27

# BRADLEY'S FUNERAL

· · · · · · · · · ·

s Melba drove off toward the highway, the officers began stringing up yellow tape around the entire crime scene. A crew would be arriving shortly to begin searching and investigating the home and property. The officers did discover a white van hidden in the garage.

They would eventually get to the bottom of all the crimes committed by Marylynn, including what happened to Ernie's mother, younger sister, Carrie, and little Bradley, and where their bodies were buried, with the help of Ernie and Thad, Carrie's diary, and Timarie's testimonies.

Marylynn was tried in court. The jury found her guilty on three counts of murder, crimes against humanity, two counts of kidnapping, two counts of false imprisonment, and several additional charges.

The Harrises had been notified of the sad fate of their son. They came to meet me in person so they could hear the whole story of what happened during the time that Bradley was imprisoned at the Myers' home. They wanted to hear every detail of how I cared for him and how much he meant to me. They wanted to hear all about how we colored together, the bedtime stories I read to him, the puzzles we assembled together and all the sweet conversations we'd had. It helped them to feel a little closer to him. Oh, how they wept... bitterly. I will never be able to forget the utter sadness and emptiness that showed in their eyes. How helpless they felt at their inability to be there to help their son when he needed them so desperately. When he had been taken initially, when he became deathly ill...they weren't there. Bradley's mother would forever blame herself.

After Bradley's body was exhumed from the bottom of the lake, his family held a funeral for him. Of course, I was there with my mom and dad along with Trish and her parents. There were pictures of Bradley displayed above his tiny casket. He looked just as I remembered him. Dark, wavy locks of hair that framed that cherubic face. Such a big, beautiful smile that showed off his adorable little dimples. Soft blue eyes that revealed his tender nature. I was unable to hold back my emotions any longer. I broke down and sobbed uncontrollably. His mother wrapped her arms around me. All she could say was, "I know, I know".

There was not a dry eye in the parlor. Everyone seemed to feel the full impact of this terrible loss.

His parents spoke on his behalf. They shared their deep love for him and how their lives would forever be changed without him. How he was one of the most animated, smart, funny, little boys they had ever known and how they were likely never to heal from this loss. They thanked me for being such a comfort and a friend to him and for loving him as I had.

It was a pleasure just to know him. His memory will always be in my heart as he was a very special chapter in my life, though much too short.

# EPILOGUE

Tiffany Sanders, still seated at the table, having finally heard the whole story blurted anxiously, "So, what then, Mom?"

She'd become so involved with the whole story, she wasn't ready for it to be over. She too, had experienced the whole gamut of emotions and felt almost as though she knew everyone involved personally.

"That's pretty much it. Well, okay...then I lived happily ever after". Tiffany smiled. "Well, there's one more thing. Have I ever mentioned to you that our Duchess is Princeton's great, great, granddaughter? Actually, I would have to look at all the pedigree papers to be sure of how many "greats" are involved.

"Really Mom?" Tiffany walked over to the back door and called Duchess. She obediently loped to the door as Tiffany motioned for her to come in. Tiffany looked down at Duchess, placed both her hands on either side of Duchess' muzzle, lifted her head so she could look her directly into her eyes and said, "Do you have any idea how special you are?" Duchess looked back up at Tiffany. She seemed to hang on every word almost as though she understood what Tiffany was saying. "You are Princeton's great granddaughter. That makes you royalty. Your great grandfather was a hero." Tiffany scratched Duchess under the chin and said, "I wish you'd told me this before. I mean...I've always loved Duchess but knowing what I know now makes her all the more special to me."

"She's every bit as intelligent, loyal and affectionate as he was.

And, she looks very much like him in color and stature. He was a beauty too, only a bit larger than Duchess. This is why I make sure to breed another generation before the current one becomes too old to breed. This is my only way of keeping Princeton with me in some small way. I will never forget him. He was my childhood hero. And just to let you know, we will be having Duchess bred in the near future so we can keep the tradition going. And NOW...I'm finished."

"Wow, Mom. You really ought to write a book about what happened. It's an amazing story. You really ought to share it with the whole world,"

"If you still want to go to the mall, I'll drive you and Kara. Agreed?"

Tiffany grinned. "Agreed'".

Author: Laurel Jackson Vance

Printed in the United States
by Baker & Taylor Publisher Services